INSPECTOR SAITO'S SMALL SATORI

Janwillem van de Wetering

BALLANTINE BOOKS • NEW YORK

Library of Congress Catalog Card Number: 84-17833

ISBN 0-345-33257-1

Saito and the Fox Girl first appeared in *Ellery Queen's Magazine*. Inspector Saito's Small Satori, Samurai Saito (as "Inspector Saito's Simple Solution"), Saito's Summary, Saito and the Shogun, Saito and the Sacred Stick, Saito's Small Oversight (as "A Small Oversight"), and Saito and the Twenty-Sen Stamp first appeared in *Alfred Hitchcock's Mystery Magazine*.

Manufactured in the United States of America

First Ballantine Books Edition: January 1987

Hailed by the *Los Angeles Times* as "one of the masters of the mystery form," Janwillem van de Wetering is the author of the widely acclaimed mystery series featuring Detective-Adjutant Grijpstra and Sergeant de Gier of Amsterdam's Murder Brigade. Now, in INSPECTOR SAITO'S SMALL SATORI, you will meet the brilliant Japanese detective Saito Masanobu, whose lightning-quick deductions and deep knowledge of Eastern culture make his cases anything but conventional. Filled with unusual characters and exotic settings, laced with humor both subtle and broad, and starring a detective who is excellent company indeed, this book will be absolute bliss for the most discriminating mystery lovers.

"A rare combination of good character development, intellectual content, humor, exotic settings, and coherent plots...These are not unfeeling, hard-bitten cops. They are sensitive, personable men of whom we grow very fond. They seem like real people and it is as much to find out more about them as to see what new plots or settings van de Wetering can come up with that we eagerly await each new book."
The Armchair Detective

"He is adept at turning a plot that can leave one guessing." *The Chicago Daily News*

"What makes this series so engaging is that the policemen are as quirky and complicated and human as the criminals."
The Washington Post

Also by Janwillem van de Wetering

OUTSIDER IN AMSTERDAM
WEED
THE CORPSE ON THE DIKE
DEATH OF A HAWKER
THE JAPANESE CORPSE
THE BLOND BABOON
THE MAINE MASSACRE
THE MIND MURDERS
THE STREETBIRD
THE BUTTERFLY HUNTER
BLISS AND BLUSTER
THE RATTLE-RAT

Nonfiction
THE EMPTY MIRROR
A GLIMPSE OF NOTHINGNESS

Children's Books
HUGH PINE
HUGH PINE AND THE GOOD PLACE
HUGH PINE IN BROOKLYN
LITTLE OWL

CONTENTS

INSPECTOR SAITO'S SMALL SATORI

INSPECTOR SAITO FELT A BIT BETTER WHEN THE CON-
stable had switched off the Datsun's siren, but just a trifle
better for his headache throbbed on. Once more he felt
sorry about having visited the Willow Quarter the night
before, and about the sixth jug of sake. He should have
remembered his limit was five jugs. But it had been a
good bar and there had been good people in the bar. And
the difference between six jugs and five jugs is only one
jug, yet that one small jug had caused the headache, which
even after sixteen hours showed no sign of abating.

He forced himself to walk over to the uniformed sergeant, a middle-aged man in a crisp green uniform waiting
under the large ornamental gate. The sergeant bowed.
Saito bowed back.

"In that direction, sir, in the alley next to the temple."

Saito grunted. There was a corpse in the alley, a female
corpse—a *gaijin* body, white, limp, and lifeless. This much

he knew from Headquarters. It was all very unfortunate, a miserable conglomeration of circumstances, all of them bad. He shouldn't have a hangover, he shouldn't have been on the night shift, and he shouldn't be trying to solve a murder case. But he *had* had too much to drink the night before, his colleague *was* ill, and there *had* been a murder. And the three events now met in the person of Saito, only a short distance from an alley between two temples in Daidharmaji, the most beautiful and revered of all temple complexes in the holy city of Kyoto.

Saito's foot stumbled over a pine root that twisted over the gravel of the path. He had to swing out his arms and then sidestep to regain his balance. He was dancing quite gracefully for a moment, but the effort exhausted him and he stopped and looked around. Daidharmaji, Temple of the Great Teaching. A gong sounded in the center of the compound and its singing metal clang filled the quiet path and was caught and held by the eighty-foot-thick mud-and-plaster walls shielding the temples and their peaceful gardens.

Saito's brain cleared and he could think for a few seconds. The Great Teaching. He remembered that these temples had but one purpose: the teaching of the truth to priests, monks, and laymen. Right now monks were sitting in meditation after having chanted to the accompaniment of the bronze gongs of the main temple. In their minds insight was supposed to develop and this insight would, in time and after much effort, rise to the surface of their beings like bubbles, or flashes of light. Enlightenment, manifested in sudden outbursts of what the teachers called *Satori*.

He smiled unhappily. Satori indeed. He recollected what

he knew about the term. Insight has to do with detachment, with the breaking of the shell in which ego hides and which it uses as a defense to hold onto its identity—to a name, to possessions, to having and being. Satori cracks the shell and explodes into freedom. By becoming less, one gains. The experience is said to be a release and leads to laughter. Monks who, through their daily discipline and meditation, manage to touch reality usually laugh or, at least, smile.

Saito sighed. All very interesting on some lofty level. Not his level, however. He was an ordinary dim-witted man, muddling about. He was muddling about now, and the sergeant was waiting, a few steps ahead. Saito nodded and limped forward.

"Did you hurt yourself, sir?"

"Just a little. I didn't see the root."

"It's a bad root, sir, but it can't be removed. It belongs to that great pine over there, a very old tree, a holy tree."

Saito followed until the sergeant stopped and began to gesture. They had come to a narrow path with some shrubbery on each side, backed by temple walls.

The sergeant pointed and stepped back. Two uniformed constables were guarding two well-pruned cherry trees.

"In there?"

"Yes, sir. Another few yards, under a bush. We haven't touched the corpse, sir."

Saito walked on, protecting his face with an arm that felt as if it was made out of hard plastic. He didn't want a branch to snap against his head. One little blow and his skull would break.

He sat on his haunches and studied the corpse. It was a woman, still young, perhaps in her late twenties. She

had long blonde hair and was dressed in white cotton
trousers and a white jacket buttoned up to the neck,
Chinese Communist style. A red scarf had been tucked
into the jacket's collar. Its color matched the stains on
the jacket. Saito produced a small flashlight and shone it
on her face. It was the sort of face seen on models in
expensive western-style fashion magazines—beautiful,
but cold, quite devoid of expression. Cool, impersonal,
and dead. He studied the slack painted mouth. Very dead.

The sergeant was hissing respectfully just behind Saito's head. The inspector straightened up. "Yes, Sergeant.
Please tell me all you know."

The sergeant checked his watch. "Ten fifteen P.M. now,
sir. Young Tanaka reported the death at nine fifty-four.
Young Tanaka lives nearby and he goes to drawing classes
in the temple at the end of this alley on the left. He said
he was going home and saw something white in the bushes.
He investigated, saw the dead person, and came to tell
us at the station."

"Person?"

"Yes, sir. He told us he had found a dead person."

"But this is a woman."

"Yes, sir. I came here with him, ran back and told my
constables where the corpse was and ordered them to
guard it, then I telephoned Headquarters."

Saito bent down and straightened up again, painfully.
"The blood seems fresh, Sergeant. I hope the doctor is
on his way. Do you know the lady?"

"Yes, sir. She studied meditation in the temple at the
end of the alley, on the right, opposite the temple where
young Tanaka learns how to draw. She is an American.
Her name is Miss Davis and she stayed at the Kyoto
Hotel. She came here most evenings, walked through this

alley on her way in and out of the compound, and hailed a taxi from the main gate, opposite our station."

"Ah. And the priest who teaches her meditation?"

"The Reverend Ohno. He has several *gaijin* as disciples. They come every weekday, in the evening, and sit in meditation from seven to nine."

"Nine o'clock," Saito said, "and then they go home?"

"Yes, sir. But the others—there are two elderly ladies and a gentleman, also old—walk another way. They take a taxi from the west gate. They don't live in such an expensive hotel as the Kyoto Hotel. Miss Davis always walked by herself. It's only a short distance to the main gate and the compound is reputed to be safe."

Saito glanced down at the sprawling corpse. "Yes. Very safe. That's a knife wound, Sergeant. Do you know of anybody walking around here at night, anybody who carries a knife?"

At least two sirens tore at the quiet cool evening and Saito's hands came up and rubbed his temples. The sirens increased in volume and stopped. The sergeant barked at one of the constables and the young man saluted and jumped away.

"Anybody with a knife, Sergeant?"

The sergeant bowed and looked sad. "Yes, sir. There are street robbers, it is true. The compound is not safe anymore. It used to be, and Miss Davis believed it to be. But..."

"But?"

"But there are young men, young men in tight trousers and leather jackets. They robbed an old man last week. The victim described the young men and I found the suspects and confronted them with the old man. He recognized the robbers but the suspects went free. There was only one witness, sir. To charge a suspect I need two witnesses."

"Were these robbers around tonight?"

"Probably, sir. When they aren't drinking or smoking the drug they roam about. They live close by. This is their territory. I will have them brought in for questioning."

"Good. And what about young Tanaka, where is he now?"

"At home, sir. I know his parents. I can call him to the station."

"Is he a good boy?"

The sergeant smiled his apology.

"Is he?"

"No, sir, and yes. We arrested him last year, and the year before. He is still young—sixteen years old. Indecent exposure, sir. But he is much better now. The priest who teaches him drawing says he has been behaving very well lately."

The constable had come back, leading a small party of men in dark suits, carrying suitcases. The men bowed at Saito and Saito returned the greeting, adjusting the depth, or lack of depth, of each bow to the colleague he was facing. The doctor grunted and asked for light. Several powerful torches lit up the grisly scene. A camera began to click. A light fed by a heavy battery was set up on a tripod.

Saito touched the sergeant's sleeve and they stepped back together. "Where is the hotel where these other Westerners stay?"

"The old *gaijin*, sir? They stay at the Mainichi."

Saito nodded. "I will go there now. And then I will come back to the station. Later on I will speak with the Reverend Ohno. Bring the young men and the boy Tanaka to the station so I can question them. Your information has been very clear. Thank you, Sergeant."

The sergeant bowed twice, deeply. "I have served in this neighborhood for many years now, sir. I try to know what goes on."

"Yes," Saito said and closed his eyes. The sergeant had spoken loudly and he had a high voice.

"I see," the old gentleman in the bathrobe said. He had knelt down on the tatami-covered floor of the hotel's reception room and seemed quite at ease on the thick straw mat. Saito sat opposite the old gentleman, with the two elderly ladies on his right in low cane chairs. They were both dressed in kimonos printed with flowers. They weren't the right sort of kimonos for old ladies to wear. Flower patterns are reserved for young girls, preferably attractive girls.

"My name is McGraw," the old gentleman said, "and my friends here are called Miss Cunningham and Mrs. Ingram. They are spending a year in Japan, and I have lived here for several years now. We are studying with the good priests of Daidharmaji."

Saito acknowledged McGraw's opening by bowing briefly.

Miss Cunningham coughed and made her thin body lean forward.

"Are you a follower of the way too, Inspector?"

"Yes, I am."

"Do you meditate?"

"No, Miss Cunningham, I do not practice. My family belongs to a temple in another part of the city. I go there with my parents on special days and the priests visit our home. That is all."

"What a pity," said Mrs. Ingram. "Meditation is such a marvelous exercise. It has done wonders for us. But you are very busy, of course. Perhaps later, when you retire?"

"Yes, Mrs. Ingram." He felt proud that he could remember the difficult names and that he was speaking English. He had studied English because he had wanted to be a police officer in Tokyo. There were many foreigners in the capital and English-speaking police detectives were rapidly promoted. But so far he had been confined within the limits of his home city, Kyoto, the city of temples.

He cleared his throat and addressed himself to McGraw. "Please, sir, what do you know about Miss Davis?"

McGraw's heavy-lidded pale-blue eyes rested on the neat impassive form of the inspector.

"May I ask, Saito-san, what sort of trouble Miss Davis is into?"

"She is dead."

While the two ladies shrieked, McGraw's eyes didn't change. They remained gentle and precise. "I see. And how did she die?"

"We are not sure yet. I would think she had been knifed."

The two ladies shrieked again, much louder. Saito closed his eyes with desperate determination.

When he left the small hotel a little while later Saito carried some information. Miss Davis had spent only two months in Japan. She was rich. Her father manufactured most of the shoe polish used in the United States. She could have lived a life of leisure, but she had not; she had been very diligent, never missing an evening's meditation at the priest Ohno's temple. She had managed to master the full lotus position, wherein both legs are crossed and the feet rest upside down on the opposite thighs. She had been in pain but she had never moved during the half-hour periods in which the two-hour sessions were divided. She had been very good indeed.

McGraw was most positive about the young woman's efforts. He himself, Miss Cunningham, and Mrs. Ingram couldn't be compared to Miss Davis. The three older students had some experience in the discipline, but even they still moved when the pain became too severe and they still fell asleep sometimes when they happened not to be in pain and Ohno-san often had to shout at them to make them wake up. Miss Davis never fell asleep. She had been an ideal student, yes, absolutely.

But McGraw knew little about Miss Davis's personal life. He didn't know how she spent her days. He had asked her to lunch once and she had accepted the invitation but never returned it. They had conversed politely but nothing of consequence. All he had learned was that she had lived in New York, held a degree in philosophy, and had experimented with drugs.

And tonight? Had he noticed anything in particular?

No. It had been an evening like the other evenings. They had sat together in Ohno's magnificent temple room. When the two hours were up and the sound of Ohno's heavy bell floated away toward the garden, they had bowed and left. McGraw had walked Miss Cunningham and Mrs. Ingram home and Miss Davis had left by herself, as usual.

Saito sat in the back of the small Datsun and asked the young constable to drive slowly. When he spied a bar, Saito asked him to stop. He got out and drank two glasses of grape juice and one glass of orange juice and swallowed two aspirin provided by the attractive hostess, who snuggled against his shoulder and smiled invitingly. Saito thanked her for the aspirin, said goodbye regretfully, and hurried back to the car.

The Datsun stopped under a blue sign with the neat characters that make up the imported word *police*. Saito marched into the station. The sergeant pointed to a door in the rear. Saito nodded before sitting down at the desk. "I'll be with you in a few minutes. After a phone call."

The doctor's hoarse voice described what Saito wanted to know. "Yes, she died of a knife wound. A downward thrust, with considerable force. The blade hit a rib but pushed on and reached the heart. Death must have been almost immediate. The knife's blade was quite long, at least three and a half inches. I can't say how wide for it moved about when it was pulled free."

"Sexual intercourse?" Saito asked.

"Not recently, no."

"Thank you. Can you connect me with whoever went through her pockets? I noticed she had no handbag."

Another voice greeted the inspector politely. "No, Inspector, there was no handbag, but the lady carried her things in the side pockets of her jacket. We found a wallet with some money, almost ten thousand yen, and a credit card. Also a key, cigarettes, a lighter, and a notebook— excuse me, sir, I have a list here. Yes, that's right, and a lipstick. That was all, sir."

"What's in the notebook?"

"Names and phone numbers."

"Japanese?"

"No, sir, American names. And the phone numbers begin with 212, 516, and 914."

Saito nodded at the telephone. "New York area codes. I have been there once. Very good, thank you."

The sergeant was waiting at the door and led Saito to a small room where two surly young men sat slumped on a wooden bench in the back. A chair had been placed opposite the bench. The sergeant closed the door and leaned against it. "The fellow on the left is called Yoshida, and the other one is Kato."

Saito was thirsty again and wondered whether he should ask the sergeant for a pot of green tea but instead he plunged right in. "O. K., you two, where were you tonight? You first—Kato, is it?"

The two young men were hard to tell apart in their identical trousers, jackets, and shirts. They even wore the same hairstyle, very short on top, very long on the sides.

"We were around."

"Where were you between nine and ten?"

They looked at each other and shrugged. "Around."

"That's bad," Saito said cheerfully. "Real bad. If no one saw you between nine and ten, you are in trouble. You may have to spend the night here, and many other nights besides. This is a nasty place, eh, Sergeant?"

"Yes, sir."

"Small cells, bad food, nothing to smoke. Do you fellows smoke?"

They nodded.

"You'll have to give it up for a while." He took a cigarette. "But I'll smoke for you. Did you go through their pockets, Sergeant?"

"Yes, sir."

"Any knives?"

The sergeant stepped out of the room and came back carrying two yellow plastic trays, neatly labeled. There

was a pack of cigarettes in each tray, plus a dirty handkerchief, a wallet, and a long knife sheathed in leather.

"Good. Please have one of your men have the knives
checked for blood."

"Blood?" the young man called Yoshida asked. "What
blood?"

"A lady's blood, a *gaijin* lady. Did you see her in the
compound tonight?"

Kato answered, "An old lady or a young lady?"

"A young lady with long blonde hair, wearing white
clothes."

"Not tonight, but we know her. She came every evening to Ohno-san's temple. She was a holy woman." He
sniggered and nudged his friend.

Saito jumped up, leaped across the room, and grabbed
Kato by the shoulders, shaking him vigorously. "What do
you mean, you punk! What do you mean?" He pushed
Kato back on the bench and stood over him, one hand
balled up.

"Nothing."

"You meant something. Tell me, or . . ." He could feel
the artificial rage turning into real rage. He would have
to watch himself.

"I just mean that maybe the lady liked the priest. Me
and Yoshida saw them together in the garden one afternoon last week, in the temple's garden."

"What were they doing?"

"Laughing, talking."

"That's all?"

"They weren't kissing," Yoshida said gruffly, "just
enjoying a good conversation."

Saito turned to the sergeant, who had returned. "Would

you ask somebody to make me a pot of tea, Sergeant? And bring a chopstick, just one."

The sergeant raised his eyebrows but bowed and left the room. He came back with the chopstick.

"Here," Saito said. "You, Kato. You are a knife fighter, eh? Here is a knife. Now attack me."

Kato hesitated and Saito waited. Kato got up and took the chopstick.

"Come on, attack me. Here I am, and you hold a knife. Show me that you can handle it."

Kato got up and the sergeant's hand dropped down and touched the revolver on his belt. The atmosphere in the room became tense. Kato spread his legs and hefted the chopstick. Saito waited, motionless. Then Kato yelled loudly and jumped. The hand holding the chopstick shot up. But Saito was no longer there—he had fallen sideways and his foot was against Kato's shin. Kato fell too. The chopstick broke on the floor. Saito helped the young man back on his feet. "Fine. Sergeant, may we have another chopstick?"

Yoshida's attack was more artful and took more time. He approached Saito, holding the chopstick low, but seemed to change his mind and feinted at the sergeant. The sergeant pulled his gun as the chopstick went for Saito's stomach, but Saito's arm effectively blocked it with a blow to Yoshida's arm, knocking it aside.

A constable brought a pot of tea. Saito poured himself a steaming cup of tea and sat sipping it, eyeing his opponents. Kato was rubbing his shin and Yoshida was massaging his wrist. "Did I hurt you?"

Both shook their heads and tried to smile.

"I didn't mean to hurt you. But carrying knives with blades longer than three inches is illegal. The sergeant will charge you and you will be kept here for the night. Perhaps I'll see you tomorrow. If you want to see me you can tell the sergeant. Good night."

He got up and went outside, beckoning the sergeant to follow him. "Now the other one, Tanaka, the boy who found the corpse."

"He is waiting in the other room, sir."

Saito smiled when he saw the boy. Young Tanaka was a good-looking young man, with a childish open face but wide shoulders and narrow hips. He wore his school uniform, and his cap was on the floor under his chair. He got up and bowed when Saito entered.

"Thank you for reporting to us tonight, Tanaka-san," Saito said, "that was very good of you. I am sorry to have you called in so late, but we have to work quickly. Did you know the *gaijin* lady at all?"

"Yes, sir, I have seen her many times. She studied at Ohno-san's temple. But I never spoke to her. And I didn't know the corpse was the *gaijin* lady's body. I was frightened, sir. I saw a body and there was nobody else around and I just ran to the police station."

"So that's why you said you saw a *person*."

"Yes, sir. I just saw the legs and a hand."

Saito tried to remember the corpse. There had been no polish on the nails, no colored polish anyway. He lowered his voice. "Now tell me, Tanaka-san, tell me and be honest. I know you have been in trouble with the police before. You know what I am referring to, don't you?"

"Yes, sir. But I don't do that anymore. I used to, but that has gone."

"What has gone?"

"The need to do that, sir."

"You are sure, are you? You were in the alley, and the

lady was in the alley. You were facing her and she was coming closer..."

"No, sir. The body was in the bushes."

Saito turned to the sergeant. "May I have a chopstick, Sergeant?"

When the sergeant returned with the chopstick Saito gave it to the boy. "Imagine this is a knife. Can you do that?"

The boy held the chopstick. "Yes, sir. It is a knife."

"And I am your enemy. I am a burglar sneaking into your room. I am going to attack you and you must kill me. Stick the knife into me. It is very important. Please do it for me."

"Like this, sir?"

The boy raised his arm high, pointing the chopstick at Saito's chest.

"Yes, you are very angry, very frightened. All you know is that you have to kill me."

The chopstick hit Saito's chest with force and broke.

"Thank you. You can go home now. Sleep well..."

When Saito left the police station, his driver came to attention and opened the rear door. The inspector shook his head. "No. I am going into the temple compound. I may be a while. You can wait in the station if you like. The tea isn't bad."

He walked until he found Ohno's temple and stopped and looked about. He could feel the quietness of hundreds of years of strong silent effort. The aspirin had dulled his headache, and his thoughts connected more easily.

The gate of the temple hadn't been locked and he walked through it.

"Good evening." The voice came from the shadows of the building.

"Good evening. My name is Saito. I am a police inspector. I have come to see the priest Ohno."

"I am Ohno. Walk up the steps and come and sit next to me."

Saito took off his shoes and walked across the polished boards of the porch. His eyes adjusted to the darkness and he could see the shape of a man sitting upright with his legs folded. Saito bowed and a cushion slid toward him. He took the cushion and sat down.

"Do you know that Miss Davis died tonight?"

"I heard."

"Who told you?"

"The old woman who cleans the temple. She heard a commotion in the alley and found out what had happened."

"The death of the *gaijin* lady is unfortunate. She was killed with a knife. We are holding several suspects."

He could see the priest's face now. Ohno was still a young man—thirty years old perhaps, or a little older. The priest wore a simple brown robe. The faint light of a half moon reflected on his shaven skull.

"Who did you arrest?"

"Two young toughs, Yoshida and Kato. They have robbed in the Daidharmaji compound before but nothing could be proved. They couldn't explain their movements at the time of Miss Davis's death. They both carried knives. We are also holding a boy called Tanaka, who reported the crime. Excuse me, do you have a telephone?"

Ohno got to his feet and led his guest inside the temple. Saito dialed. A man in the laboratory answered.

"The knives? They both fit the wound but so would a

million other knives. And they are both clean, no traces of blood."

"Whoever did it could have cleaned the knife afterward."

"He could. If he did, he did a good job."

"Thank you."

The priest invited Saito into his study and an old woman made them tea. Saito sipped slowly, enjoying the rich bitter taste.

"Very good tea."

"A present from Mrs. Ingram. I couldn't afford it myself."

"You have only foreign disciples?"

"Yes. When *gaijin* come to Daidharmaji, the chief abbot usually sends them to me. I am the only priest who speaks reasonably good English. I spent several years in a temple in Los Angeles as the assistant to the teacher there."

"I see. Did you get to know Miss Davis well?"

"A little. She was a dedicated woman, very eager to learn."

"Did she learn anything?"

Ohno smiled. "There is nothing to learn. There is only to unlearn."

Saito shook his head.

"You don't agree?"

"I have no wisdom," Saito said. "I am a policeman; my level of investigation is shallow. I have small questions and need small answers. Yoshida and Kato weren't helpful. The boy Tanaka tried, but he couldn't tell me much. Mr. McGraw and the old ladies who study with you tried to clarify my confusion. But I am still confused and now I have come to see you."

"I know the two young men, Yoshida and Kato," Ohno

said. "I know their parents too—they often come to these temples. The boys have lost their way, but only for the time being. They will find the way again. They may have robbed people but they have never killed anyone. They watch movies and try to imitate images of what they think is admirable."

"In the movies many images get killed. Yoshida and Kato carry knives, killing knives with slits in the sides so that the blood will drain easily."

"They didn't kill tonight."

"And the boy Tanaka, do you know him too?"

"Very well. When his mind was sick, his parents came to see me. They live close by and they often bring gifts to this temple. They knew the priest who lived here before and now they come and visit me. The boy was mad, they said, but I didn't think so. The boy came too sometimes— he liked to help me in the garden. He placed the rocks and we planted moss."

"He would show himself when he met women, right here, in this holy compound."

"I know."

"You don't think that is a bad thing to do?"

"It is embarrassing, for the women and for the boy himself. But he had a need to reveal himself to that which he loved. I wanted to help him but didn't know what to do and spoke to the old priest in the temple next door. Young Tanaka likes to paint and draw, and the old priest is an accomplished artist. So we agreed that he would try to lead Tanaka away from his compulsion. Since then the boy's trouble has faded away. There have been no more complaints."

Saito got up. He wanted to say something noncommittal before he left. He looked around and saw several cameras on a shelf and another on the floor. "Do you like photography, Ohno-san?"

"Yes, it is my hobby." The priest picked up the camera. "I use a new method now. I make instant photographs and if I succeed in obtaining a well-balanced picture, I try again with a conventional camera that can be adjusted to a fine degree of perception. One day when you have time you should come and see some of my photographs— if you are interested, that is."

"I would very much like to. Thank you."

Saito looked at his watch. It was past one o'clock but he might as well go on. He was very close now, but there were still important questions.

The temple next door was dark and the gate had been locked, but he found a side door and made his way into the courtyard, using his flashlight. He took off his shoes and climbed the steps and knocked on the door of the main building. Within seconds a light came on inside and shuffling steps approached. The priest was old and bent— and sleepy.

"Yes?"

Saito showed his identification. "Inspector Saito, Criminal Investigation Department. I am sorry, sir, but I have to bother you for a few minutes. May I come in?"

"Of course. I heard about the lady's death. Most regrettable. Please come in, Inspector-san."

In view of the late hour, Saito decided that it would be impolite to be polite. He came to the point.

"You are teaching a boy called Tanaka?"

"That is correct."

"He draws and paints. Please tell me what his favorite subjects are."

"Women. He only draws women. I don't allow him to

paint yet. He sketches. I showed him copies of famous paintings and he seemed most interested in portraits of Kwannon, the goddess of compassion. He has been drawing her for months now and doesn't tire."

Saito smiled. "Tanaka-san is in love with the goddess?"

The priest looked serious. "Very much so. And that is good for the time being. I want him to continue, to approach perfection. Later he will see that her real shape is truly perfect and then perhaps he will meet and know her. But first he must do this. He is talented. I am grateful he was brought to me."

"May I see the drawings?"

"Surely. Follow me, please."

The sketches were all in the same vein, although the postures and moods of the divine model were different. The boy clearly had only one type of woman in mind, and the woman was Japanese, with a long narrow face, thick black hair, a small nose, and enormous slanting eyes.

"Thank you."

"Not at all."

"One last question, sir. Do you know Ohno-san well?"

The old priest nodded.

"Does Ohno-san engage in any of the martial sports? Judo? Sword fighting? Bowshooting, perhaps?"

The old priest tittered. "Oh, no. Ohno-san likes to fuss in his garden, to make photographs, and to meditate, in that order. He once came to help me chop some wood for my bathhouse. He broke two axe handles in one hour. I had no more axes so we had tea instead. No, Ohno-san is, shall we say, a little clumsy?"

Nearly five minutes passed before Saito could bring himself to walk through Ohno's gate again. He found the priest where he had found him before, on the porch. Saito didn't say anything but sat down.

"Yes?"

"I am sorry, I have come to arrest you."

Ohno didn't reply. Saito sat quietly.

Several minutes passed.

"Please come with me, Ohno-san."

The priest turned and faced the inspector. "No. I will have to ask you a favor. Let me go inside and please wait half an hour. I will leave a confession and you can close your case."

Saito smiled, but the smile was neither positive nor negative. It was very quiet on the porch.

Ohno cleared his throat. "Would you mind explaining why you chose me?"

"Because you killed her. She was killed by an amateur, by someone who doesn't know how to handle a knife. A knife fighter will hold his weapon low and thrust upward, so that the knife pierces the soft skin of the belly and its point will travel upward, behind the ribs. To stab downward is silly—the ribs protect the heart. Much unnecessary force is needed. And the attacker who holds his knife high has no defense; his own body is left open."

"Many people walk through this compound. Most of them do not know how to handle a knife."

"That is not true. There are very few people about after nine o'clock. Even when we found the dead woman a crowd didn't gather. And whoever killed Miss Davis either hated her or was frightened of her. To hate or to fear takes time. The feeling isn't born overnight. Miss Davis only spent a few months in Japan and kept herself apart. The only person she involved herself with was you. You were her teacher. She came here every night. But she also came during the day. Did you sleep with her, Ohno-san?"

The priest's head jerked forward briefly. "I did."

"She seduced you?"

The head jerked again.

"She was in love with you?"

Ohno's even white teeth sparkled briefly in the soft moonlight.

"No. To love means to be prepared to give. She wanted to have. And she wanted me to give to her. The way has many secrets, many powers. Our training, when practiced properly, is complete. It is also slow, unbearably slow. Miss Davis comes from a country that believes in quick results. Americans are capable of great effort, but they want rewards. She suspected that I knew something and she wanted what I knew."

"You were teaching her meditation. You were giving."

"Yes. But meditation takes forever, or so she began to believe. She wanted to be initiated, to be given powers. I told her my rank was too low, my development too minute. Only a true teacher can pass a student. This temple is a little school for beginners, for toddlers. The abbot knows I have disciples and he watches them. He will take over when he feels that the disciples are ready. Mr. McGraw is sometimes allowed to see the abbot: He has learned much—he has learned to be modest. Miss Davis had learned to be the opposite."

"She tried to force you?"

"Yes."

"How?"

"I am a weak man, a silly man. She began to visit me during the day. I have lived in America and I am very proud of my experience with foreigners. We flirted. Then we slept together."

"In the room where we were earlier on tonight?"

"Yes."

"The room where you have your cameras?"

"Yes. The camera can be set so that it goes off after several seconds. I showed her how. She laughed and set it and pressed herself against me. We had no clothes on. The camera clicked. She took the photograph with her. I didn't understand what she meant to do. I thought it was a joke."

"She threatened to show the photograph to the abbot?"

"Yes. Today. She came to see me this morning. She said she was prepared to continue her meditation practice for a year, but she wanted something right now. Some power. That was all she wanted—not insight, just power. She said I knew about the secret initiations and that I must make her break through. I told her we have no secret initiations. I told her that perhaps in Tibet they do, but not here."

"She planned to visit the abbot tonight?"

"Tomorrow. I had to stop her."

Saito waited. "And the abbot, what would he have done?"

"He would have sent me away. And rightly so, for I have failed. I am only a low-ranking priest. My training has hardly begun. That I am allowed to teach meditation to beginners is a great honor. I am not worthy of the honor."

Ohno's voice dropped and Saito had to strain his ears to hear the priest's words through the chirping of the cicadas.

"Tonight," Ohno said, "I watched her walk through the

gate. I ran through the garden and climbed the wall so that I would be waiting for her when she turned the corner of the temple wall and the alley. I had taken a knife from the kitchen. I put myself in her way and showed her the knife. I asked her to give me the photograph. She laughed and tried to push me aside. I became very angry. I don't think I intended to kill her, I only meant to threaten. But her laugh infuriated me."

"Do you have the photograph?"

"Yes. I don't remember how I got it. I must have taken it from the pocket of her jacket."

"And now you plan to kill yourself," Saito said pleasantly.

"Yes."

"But how can you continue your training when you are dead? Isn't this life supposed to be the ideal training ground and isn't whatever comes afterward a period of rest in which nothing can be achieved? You may have to wait a long time before you are given another chance. Is this not so?"

The dark shape next to Saito moved. "Yes."

"I don't know anything," Saito said. "But priests sometimes come to my house to burn incense in front of the family altar and to chant the holy sermons. I have listened. Isn't that what they say? What you say?"

"Yes."

"And if you come with me, if you allow yourself to be arrested and to face the court and be convicted and spend time in jail, doesn't that mean that your training will continue? That you can go on with your practice? And won't the abbot, who is a master and your teacher, come and visit you or send messages, and help you along?"

"Yes."

"And isn't it true that we all fail? And that failure is never definite? That we can always correct our situation, no matter how bad it seems to be?"

"Yes."

Saito thought he had said enough. He was tired of listening to his own voice. He brought out a cigarette and lit it. Ohno's hand reached out and Saito gave him the cigarette and lit another. They smoked together. The two stubs left the porch at the same moment and sparked away as they hit the wet moss of the garden.

They walked to the gate slowly, two men strolling through the peaceful night.

"I was worried when you said you suspected Tanaka," Ohno said. "He is a nice boy."

"Yes," Saito said. "He was the most likely suspect, but something didn't fit. Indecent exposure is an act of surrender, not of aggression. I would have arrested him if he had drawn the face or body of Miss Davis. But his fantasies are centered on the beauty of our own women. I checked just now at your neighbor's temple. Miss Davis was beautiful, but not to young Tanaka. I don't think she was even female in his eyes."

"She was in mine."

Saito didn't answer. They had passed through the main gate and reached the car. Saito leaned inside and touched the horn. The driver appeared immediately from the station.

"Headquarters, please. This venerable priest is coming with us."

"Sir." The driver bowed to Ohno. Ohno bowed back.

Saito felt pleased. He had solved the case quickly, discreetly. This could be the credit that would get him transferred to the capital. He grinned but the grin froze halfway. He tried to analyze his state of mind but he was bewildered. The more he probed, the emptier his mind seemed.

He felt the priest's presence and then his own hand reached out and touched the wide sleeve of Ohno's robe.

"Yes," Ohno said, "You were right, Inspector-san. It was silly of me to consider my shame and to respond to that shame. I am what I am and I will continue from the point where I find myself. The point happens to be bad, that is all. There will be good points later on, and they won't matter so much either. *Ha!*"

Saito grinned. The priest's words had helped him to make the grin break through, the priest's words and the strange power of quietness he had felt seeping into his being while he wandered among the temples of Daidhar-maji. And he realized that he didn't care about his successful investigation or about the forthcoming praise of his superiors or about the possibility of a transfer to the capital. The priest's shame was as much of an illusion as his own fame. He felt much relieved, lightheaded. The grin spread over his face. "*Ha!*" The laugh was as carefree as Ohno's laugh had been.

"So . . ." Ohno said.

"So nothing!" Saito replied.

The car took a sharp turn and they fell into each other's arms. They laughed together while the embrace lasted.

At Headquarters, the priest was taken to a cell and Saito accompanied him. He waited while the constable locked the heavy door. Ohno bowed. Saito bowed. They straightened up and studied each other's smile through the bars of the cell door.

"You understood something, didn't you, Inspector-san?"

"Oh, yes," Saito said softly. "Yes, I think I did."

"Oh, yes," Ohno whispered. "And it had nothing to do with you or me or even poor Miss Davis."

"No, it didn't." Saito nodded and gazed at Ohno before turning and following the constable out of the cell block. He felt very tired, so tired that he was hallucinating. He wasn't walking through a dimly lit concrete corridor but floating in a lake of light. The light began to fade as he approached his house and he found that he was shaking his head and talking to himself.

2

SAMURAI SAITO

THE LIP WAS STILL SWELLING. THE INSPECTOR WAS amazed. Surely any phenomenon has its reasonable limit. His lip had to be an exception to a common rule, or the insect that had caused the protuberance, at first limited to the far left side of Saito's mouth, but now spread out to the other side.

He observed his face in a mirror he had improvised out of the glass top of his desk and a piece of dark cardboard. The Zulu warrior effect. All he needed was a bone to stick through the lip. He looked perfectly ridiculous.

Saito pulled the piece of cardboard away and dropped it into his wastepaper basket. The affliction would be temporary and shouldn't interfere with his good mood. He had done well that morning. He had managed to get up early and had breakfasted and shaved at leisure. He had even done some useful work: raking the small yard in front of his garage. Now he was in his room at Kyoto Police Headquarters, the first room he had ever had to himself in the big forbidding building. He had, in a way, been promoted. He was still an ordinary inspector, of course, but he had been nudged up the ladder. And the door had his name on it—SAITO MASANOBU, in bright brown characters.

He sat down and frowned. It would be nice if he had something to do. He frowned again. What was wrong with asking, with framing a desire? He closed his eyes and concentrated, opened them again, and smiled—with his upper lip only. Not only had he asked, he had specified his request. The words had flashed onto the screen of his mind. "I, Inspector Saito, want something to do, something worthy of my intelligence."

The inspector was a great believer in the power of positive thought. But forty minutes passed and his telephone didn't even ring. Meanwhile he busied himself. First he tried to scratch his lip. Then he made a pot of strong tea on the small hotplate on his desk. Finally he read his newspaper.

There was a knock on the door.

"Yes?"

"Sir," the constable at the door said, "there's a lady in the corridor. The desk sergeant has sent her upstairs because he doesn't want to listen to her any more. Sergeant Fujiyama says she is confused, her complaints are unclear, but she refuses to be sent away. All the other inspectors are busy, sir. Would you—?"

"Yes," Saito said pleasantly, "I would. Bring her in. But wait just a minute, Constable, just a minute."

The constable stood at attention while Saito lit a cigarette. If the desk sergeant said the woman was confused, then she undoubtedly was. Saito hadn't dealt much with confused women so far, but the constable was more experienced. He was an older man with a thin, wizened, under-standing sort of face and bright eyes. Saito remembered his own age: twenty-six. He also remembered that it wasn't a good idea to listen to complainants with no one else present.

"Bring the lady in and stay with us."

"Sir!" the constable barked, and marched away, leaving the door open.

He was back at once, followed by a slender girl in a white kimono printed with a pattern of delicate blue flowers. She made a series of bows, each one deeper than the last. Her voice belied her slight appearance. It was low, a little husky even. Saito noted the large eyes, slanting steeply. Although she was dressed conservatively—the flower pattern suited her age, which couldn't have been much more than twenty—her hair, cut rather short, betrayed a more modern influence.

"Excuse me," the girl was saying. "Please. I am causing so much trouble today. Please excuse me."

Saito indicated two chairs. She sat down carefully and folded her hands. The constable bowed briefly, took one step back, bent his knees and sat down too. He looked most efficient in his crisp olive-green uniform.

The girl glanced at the constable's large revolver, protruding almost obscenely from an impeccably polished holster. "Yes," she said softly, "I did not want to bother the police, but what can I do? The boots are stolen and cannot be replaced. I must get them back—my grandfather is terribly unhappy. He is old, you see, and ill, and I look after him. There are only the two of us. The boots remind him of better days. He was a corporal once in the Imperial Army, and he was very brave and commanded many men. He fought in China. And he used to wear these high boots, in the old-fashioned style, with separate compartments for the big toes.

"He was always telling me about the boots. He lost them when he returned to Japan. But when we were in Kobe last month he saw a new pair in a store window. The price was high, but I had the money, and we bought them. And now they are gone. I already telephoned the store, but they are sold out now and they say that they do not know where others are available. My grandfather is so sad. He wore them in the garden all the time and he marched around and sang and gave orders. He is old now, and he has so few pleasures left."

"Ah," Saito said. "I am sorry to hear that. How did the boots disappear?"

"You must excuse me. I am so silly. This morning I had to go into the garden to get some radishes for breakfast. It was wet and I put grandfather's boots on. I shouldn't have but I did. And then a man came jumping across the fence and stole the boots."

Saito had been fingering his lip again, but stopped, trying to visualize the scene. "But you were wearing the boots! Did the fellow take them from your feet?"

She nodded. "Yes. You see, he didn't just come for the boots. He must have seen me bending over to pick the radishes. I wasn't dressed properly. I thought nobody could see me. He leaped across the fence and grabbed me, then he turned me around and pushed me into the tool shed. I screamed but my grandfather is deaf and there are no close neighbors. There's some mulch in the shed and he told me to lie down, but I bit him and yelled and yelled. Then he slapped my face and I fell, half out of the shed. I felt him tugging at the boots and when he got them off he ran away with them."

Saito gasped. "But that's rape, attempted rape anyway, Miss—what's your name?"

"Washino."

"—Attempted rape, Washino-san. Here this ruffian tries to rape you on your own property and you come here prattling about boots!"

She looked at him, her eyes sad and forlorn.

"Yes, sir," the constable said, "that's why the desk sergeant lost his patience. She isn't interested in pressing the rape charge. She only wants the boots back. The boots are worth perhaps six thousand yen, not a big sum. If we do find the culprit and charge him with theft, the court will not be interested. The sergeant did tell Washino-san to go away but she wouldn't, and so—"

"So you brought her to me," Saito said, feeling his lip. He winced.

"Did a deerfly bite you?" the girl asked.

"I don't know. A bee, perhaps, or a wasp. Something big. I never noticed the sting. It must have happened this morning when I was raking the yard; but I didn't notice because I was so busy. It hurts."

She was looking through her bag. "Here, try this. It is for dry skin. It will make the lip less irritated."

Saito studied the object she held out to him. It looked like a lipstick. Perhaps the crazy girl was trying to play a joke on him. "No, thank you, Miss. It'll pass, whatever it is. Well, you've heard what the sergeant said and now you've heard what the constable said. My colleagues are right. The court will throw the case out unless you accuse the suspect of attempted rape."

She dropped the stick back into her bag and bent her head. "Please, sir, please help me. You are the police. You can find the boots. You're an officer. You have many men under you, many cars. I see them everywhere. You can find the young man and make him give you back the boots so that grandfather can walk in the garden again and sing to himself. It will stop his pains. He's ill. He hasn't very long to live. I can't bear to see him unhappy." The vibration of her low voice filled the small room. Saito's spine tingled. The constable shifted on his chair.

"Don't you want us to arrest the suspect?" Saito asked.

"No, sir. I have no time to go to court, and if I take the time I may lose my job. I am a waitress in the Lotus Pond Restaurant. The owner says I work well and he may put me in charge of the other girls. But if he hears that I am in trouble, that I may have been raped, he will tell me to go away. He's very refined, very proper. He must not hear about this. I just want grandfather's boots back, that's all."

Saito groaned. He avoided the girl's steady gaze and his eyes rested on a file. He had put the file on his desk, meaning to look through it sometime. It contained his diploma and other papers. It wasn't so long ago that he had passed his inspector's examination. One of the important questions he had answered to the satisfaction of the officers facing him across the brocade-covered table was, "What is the task of the police?"

He had given the textbook reply: "The task of the police is to maintain order and to extend help to those in need of help."

There had been further questions as to the philosophical implications and historical background of the task of the police. The officers had nodded briefly when he had told them that the state, represented by its servants, the police, maintains order so that the citizens can go about their lawful business and that the samurai, the noble warriors of the past, had always defended the rights of the people.

"Yes," Saito said. "Very well, Miss. Where do you live?"

The address meant nothing to him and he found his map and unfolded it. The girl indicated an area in the extreme north, where the city petered out into fields and country lanes.

"I know that lane," the constable said. "There's just one house. I used to go fishing in a pond nearby when we still lived in the north."

"That's right. There's only our house."

"Describe your assailant, Miss."

"But you will not arrest him, please."

"No, but I must ask him to return the boots. If I don't know who he is I can't ask him."

"He is young, about twenty years old, I think. He has some hair on his face, like he hasn't shaved for a while. He's missing a tooth in the middle."

"Long hair?"

"No, very short. He had a cap on but it fell off."

"Do you have the cap?"

"No, but he left his shoes. Excuse me, I put them in the corridor."

She got up and fetched a parcel wrapped in dark cloth. She folded the cloth back and put a pair of sneakers on Saito's desk. The sneakers were old and torn and the short zippers on the sides no longer worked.

"And how did he leave? On foot?"

"On a motorcycle. I didn't see it. Our fence is rather overgrown and I am not tall. But when he left I heard an engine."

"What was the sound like?"

She smiled. "Do you want me to make the sound?"

"Please."

She giggled and covered her mouth with her hand.

"Go ahead, Miss."

"Burrum! Burrum! Bur*RUM*!"

The third "burrum" was on a higher pitch than the first two.

Saito nodded. "A motorcycle, a 350cc no doubt. A racing machine, highly geared. They are very popular nowadays, and expensive. How was the man dressed?"

"Tight jeans, a leather belt with a big brass buckle, and a short black-leather jacket."

"Do you have a telephone, Miss?"

"No."

"All right. We have your address. You'll hear from us."

She left, muttering her thanks and bowing. The sneakers were still on Saito's desk. The constable closed the door behind her and stood at attention.

"Sit down, Constable. Let me think."

Saito got up and walked over to the small bookcase he had stocked the previous day with the books he had studied for his inspector's examination. He picked up a thin volume and flipped through its pages.

"This is an interesting book, Constable," he said. "It is called *Parallel Cases Under the Pear Tree*, a classical Chinese text on detection and jurisprudence. One hundred and forty-four cases solved and judged by famous magistrates. Ah, here is what I am looking for."

He cleared his throat. "'*A married woman was washing clothes on the bank of a river. There came a traveler on horseback who violated her and rode away after he had changed his old boots for her new ones. The woman went to the prefect. The prefect summoned all the old women of the city. He showed them the old boots, saying falsely: "A man on horseback was robbed with violence on the road. These are his boots. Is there not a relative of him among you?" An old woman wailed: "My son!" Thus the criminal was found and arrested.'"*

Saito looked at the constable. "Have you listened?"

"Yes, sir."

"What did you think?"

"When did that happen, sir?"

Saito looked at the book. "During the Ch'i Dynasty. That would have been around the year 550. The prefect became a prince. Prince Ch'ieh. A famous statesman in his later days, I believe."

The constable bowed briefly in deference to the early date and noble rank. "But we cannot imitate the prince's method, sir. There are a million people in Kyoto—more now. Somebody told me that many have been added since the last count. We cannot show the sneakers to all the old women of Kyoto."

Saito replaced the book. "True, Constable. Times change. But there's something here. The minute I heard you say 'boots' I thought of the case solved by Prince Ch'ieh. Then when the girl said that the villain also tried to rape her I couldn't believe the coincidence. There's really nothing new under the sun. But you are right, we cannot summon all the mothers of Kyoto. We need more information so that our field of investigation is narrowed."

"The criminal will be a member of a motorcycle gang, sir."

"Yes. Usually these louts operate in groups. There are many such gangs, isn't that so?"

"Several, sir. But there's only one in the north. Each gang has its own district."

"Good. Do you know where they gather?"

"In the mountains, sir. There are many strange types out there. Hermits, monks, woodcutters, hunters—but also bandits. I'm glad we moved to the city, for my wife was always frightened when she was alone. A gang used to race down the lane where we lived. A colleague once took part in a raid against those fellows. An informer told his superior officer that the gang had moved into a deserted temple compound, a ruin. Perhaps the temple was once a monastery. It's well placed strategically, on the top of a hill, with a clear view on all sides. The gang must have seen the police approaching and got away in time. They are dangerous when cornered. They once attacked a highway patrol—one of the constables was badly wounded, but there were no arrests."

Saito sat down. "We'll have to go out there and get into the compound somehow. I am sure it can be done. I don't see any other way of retrieving Washino-san's grandfather's boots, do you?"

The constable began to cough.

"Don't you think so, Constable?"

"Excuse me, sir. Perhaps not, sir. There's no charge. The woman doesn't want to go to court. To go to the gang's hideout would mean to go in force, and for that you will need permission from a chief inspector. It would have to be properly organized. Many men would be involved."

"Yes," Saito said thoughtfully. "Yes, I see what you mean. What do you advise?"

"Perhaps the inspector-san should not deal with this unfortunate business."

"Yes. And the boots? The old grandfather who is ill and in pain?"

"The inspector-san should forget the matter, sir. The desk sergeant will be needing me, Saito-san."

Saito paced the room after the constable had left. It was true there was nothing to be done in his official capacity, but he was also a private individual. Private individuals have many opportunities, especially if their actions involve no one but themselves. Private individuals aren't hemmed in on all sides by police regulations.

He was home a quarter of an hour later, looking at the big Honda motorcycle in the rear of his garage. He had owned the Honda for several years now and taken good care of it. It was still fast. He kicked the starter and the heavy twin cylinders purred. He turned the key and ran into the house, got out of his dark suit, and tore off his tie. He put on a pair of torn jeans and a disreputable cloth windbreaker, then rummaged about in a drawer and found a little leather cap. He also found a pink scarf and knotted it around his neck. Then he studied the map again.

The constable had pointed out the location of the temple compound, pretending to believe that the inspector was merely curious. The desk sergeant had come over to see what the inspector and the constable were doing, but by then the constable's finger had slipped to the center of the city and the two men were discussing traffic problems. Saito grinned and quickly felt his lip again. It didn't itch anymore, but it still hurt. He looked at the mirror in the bedroom, then looked away again. He was a monstrosity.

His automatic pistol was on the bureau, complete with shoulder holster and straps. Should he take it with him? He wouldn't use it of course, but it would give him confidence. Its magazine held sixfold death, sure death, for Saito knew how to handle the gun. He had been well trained. No. He opened a drawer and dropped the pistol on a stack of shirts.

He ran down the steps, trying to whistle. The whistle wouldn't pass his lip so he hissed instead. He remembered the noble warrior blood that flowed in his veins and saw the stern face of his dead grandfather, a vice-admiral of the Imperial Navy, honorably killed in action during the last year of World War II, smiling down at him encouragingly. Obeying the call of justice, latter-day samurai Saito ran to the stable to fetch his trusted steed.

The Honda was ready, gleaming in the light of the garage's single light bulb. He took out his wallet and slid it into a tear in the saddle's lining. The sneakers left by Washino-san, tied by their laces, adorned his shoulder. He brought down his foot ferociously and the Honda's engine roared in response. Within the next few minutes he passed three orange traffic lights. Samurai are good men, but they are also rather wild and they tend to ignore minor restrictions.

The city's heavy traffic stayed behind when he reached Kyoto's northern outskirts. There were only buses now, and small three-wheeled trucks and even horse-drawn carts carrying rows of wooden buckets filled with human manure. The Honda performed well. He found the lane where Washino-san lived and rode slowly. She wouldn't be home yet—the streetcar didn't go that far and the buses were only scheduled at one-hour intervals. She might have had to walk. There were lilac trees growing from the garden onto the sidewalk. He saw the spot where the ruffian had scaled the fence, indicated by broken twigs and a split board.

He revved the engine as a salute to Washino-san's honesty, made a sharp right turn, and found the highway leading to the mountain pass. After another few miles, he took a left. But he had forgotten his directions and had to stop a few times to check his map.

It was half an hour before he saw the temple on the hill, or what was left of it. The clay outer walls of the compound had been eaten away by a hundred years of rain and wind, and the large sloping roof of the main building had partially caved in. Wildflowers grew on the road leading to the sagging gate and the vast courtyard was overgrown with knee-high thorny weeds. There were rough paths through the wilderness, however, made by feet and tires. Nobody seemed to be about, but a clothes-line sported some gaily colored shirts. He switched the engine off, kicked the Honda on its heavy metal strut, and took the sneakers off his shoulder.

When he walked to the temple's main door two men rushed him and grabbed his arms. They frog-marched him into the building.

"Easy," Saito said.

"Easy yourself. What do you want here?"

Three other young men were waiting for him inside. He was pushed against a wall and his pockets were quickly searched. A dirty handkerchief, a clasp knife, a packet of cigarettes, and a dented lighter joined the sneakers on the floor. A rough hand grabbed the collar of his jacket, yanking him back, and he turned and faced his opponents. He was angry by now, and red in the face, spitting his words. "You swine! Can't you see I am a friend? I came here to do one of your gang a favor, but now I'll say nothing. Look at his shoes. You know the shoes, don't you?"

"Taro's shoes," a tubby fellow said. "How did you get them?"

"I won't tell you."

"O.K. You're clean, but we've got to be careful. There are some that don't like us and they may send spies."

"A spy on a motorcycle?"

"Could be. We've got to be careful. Everybody gets the same treatment at first. You got no papers? No money?"

"Maybe I have. Maybe I left them somewhere. Are you the boss?"

The tubby fellow nodded and sat down on his haunches. His round belly hung over his belt. He was barefoot and a towel was wrapped around his neck. "You came early. I was just going to take my bath."

Saito checked his watch. "Early? It's almost eleven."

The tubby fellow laughed. "That's early for us. We live at night. Don't you?"

"Sure."

"What's wrong with your mouth?"

Saito touched his lip. "Oh, that? A fight. Because of your fellow."

"How come?"

"You're through with the rough stuff now?"

"Yes. You're a guest."

"I am riding through town," Saito said, gesturing widely, "looking for a bar, you know? And I find one. Last night nothing happens so I need a little strong stuff today. I go into the bar and a fight starts just as I come in. Your fellow and the owner are pushing and shoving. I don't know what the fight is about but your fellow looks like a brother so I hang around. I think maybe the owner doesn't like Taro—that's his name, right?"

"Yes."

"—Doesn't like Taro and wants to throw him out. So

I help brother Taro a little bit and then the owner's friends come in. It turns into a big fight."

"Taro fights good."

"I fight good too, but there are six on the other side. And by and by the police come. The owner says that Taro has stolen money from the bar, and the police find money on Taro. A lot of bills, all folded in half. The owner says he always folds his money before he puts it into the till. So Taro gets handcuffed. They come for me too and go through my pockets, but I have no big money—just a little, my own money. The owner says he knows Taro, he's hung around there before. He says he doesn't know me. Taro says he doesn't know me. I said I was doing nothing, but when somebody hits me I defend myself. Then Taro stumbles and falls and I help him up. 'Go tell 'em,' he whispers, 'temple in the mountains, north.' So I make it out here. I've never been here but I asked somebody where the temple in the north is and he told me."

"How'd you get Taro's shoes?"

"He lost them during the fight. I found them when the police left. So I put them in the saddlebag and here they are."

"So they got old Taro, hey?" the tubby fellow said. "That's bad. And he was riding my new Suzuki. That's bad too. Did you see the Suzuki maybe?"

"No."

"No? But it must have been outside the bar."

Saito thought quickly. "It was the Rising Moon Bar, behind the second bridge, in the Willow Quarter. That's in an alley, you can't park nothing there. Maybe the Suzuki was around the corner, in the avenue."

"You can go pick it up, chief," a young man said.

The tubby fellow shrugged. "Without a key? Taro has the key. I can pick it up in the truck but the truck has gone to town. To get some beer, I hope. When they come back tonight we can go and find the Suzuki. We've got to be careful. The police get suspicious when they see a motorcycle in a truck."

Saito picked up his belongings and lit a cigarette. He nodded. "Yes, tonight is better."

"Thanks for coming," the tubby fellow said, "and sorry about messing you around. You want some lunch?"

"No, I've got things to do. But I'd like to come back."

"Come tomorrow. Friday night is party night. It'll last all weekend, maybe longer if the beer holds out. You don't have to bring nothing, not this time. Or next time either. What gang are you with?"

"No gang," Saito said sadly. "I've been away in Tokyo— just got back. In Tokyo I was with the Skulls and Bones."

The tubby fellow smiled. "Good. Maybe you can teach us some tricks. The Tokyo gangs have fun."

"Tomorrow then," Saito said. "Are you fellows going to see Taro?"

"Not in jail, we won't. He'll come out again."

Saito broke into a sweat when he rode through the gate. They could have caught him out so easily. Why did he have to make that comment about eleven o'clock not being early? But they hadn't seemed to notice. And the absence of Taro's motorcycle was another trap. He had dodged out of that one in the nick of time. He hadn't thought of Taro's bike. A new Suzuki. Pity he didn't know the color. But to ask would have involved too much risk. He thought of the main danger he had faced. Taro could either have been in the temple or arrived while he had been talking to the gang. If they'd found him out they might have killed him. But he hadn't been found out. Thanks to luck, or to Kwannon, the smiling goddess of compassion and the patron saint of the samurai. Taro was probably still in town, having a few beers after his adventure of the morning or roaming about the Willow Quarter, looking for a prostitute. But Taro would come back. All he had to do now was wait.

He found a good spot at the side of the road and sat on a rock beside the Honda. After a while he got up and checked the gas in his tank. There wasn't much. He went back to his rock and smoked. Once in a while a car passed. The narrow path leading to the hills and the temple beyond was quite invisible.

The afternoon passed slowly. Saito became thirsty, then hungry. He had run out of cigarettes. He forced himself to stay awake and alert.

Dinnertime had come and gone when he heard the whine of the Suzuki. It was at a considerable distance, but the hills echoed the high-pitched gurgle of the small but speedy machine. Saito jumped up and started the Honda. He could hear the Suzuki downshift to climb the steep slope around the corner. He turned the Honda around and drove off. The speedometer touched fifty-five when the Suzuki tried to overtake him. He opened the throttle completely and the Honda nearly jumped from under him. He stayed next to the Suzuki. Its rider looked at him. Saito shouted and the rider shouted back. Saito saw the missing tooth. The rider had to be Taro. Saito glanced down and saw the boots. His hand shot out and made contact with Taro's shoulder.

The Honda rode alone while the Suzuki swerved and hit the soft shoulder of the road. Saito braked and looked back. Taro was struggling to maintain control, but the Suzuki was falling over. Taro jumped, rolled over, and landed on his feet.

Saito stopped, parked the Honda, and waited. Taro came running at him and assumed the judo posture, arms dangling, head down, legs apart. Taro yelled as he ran, the high yell of the karate fighter. He was close enough now and Saito stepped aside, almost casually hitting Taro's head as he flashed past. Taro ran on until he crashed into the Honda. He tried to hold on to the heavy motorcycle, but his legs folded and he crumpled to the ground.

Saito ambled toward him and knelt, pulling off one boot, then the other. He sat down and removed his own shoes. He slipped into the boots. Then he got up, picked up Taro, and dragged him into the weeds on the lower bank.

When he turned around a long low green-and-white Toyota was parked behind him. There were three policemen in the cruiser. The driver leaned out of his open window. "What happened?"

"An accident."

"Get out, men," the driver said. His sleeve showed the stripes of a sergeant. The two constables tumbled out of the cruiser. "Check them both."

"Papers," one of the constables barked.

"They're in my motorcycle."

"Go get them. I'll go with you. No tricks now."

Saito pulled his wallet out of the saddle of the Honda. The constable read the driving license and compared the photograph. "Saito, eh? What do you do for a living, Saito?"

"Nothing right now. I'm looking for a job."

"A bum, eh? Let's see the registration."

The registration was in order and the constable reluctantly returned the wallet.

"This fellow is out, Sergeant," the other constable was saying.

The sergeant clambered out of the cruiser and nudged Taro's immobile body with his boot. Taro opened one eye.

The sergeant kicked him. "Up!"

Taro was helped to his feet by the constables. He pointed at Saito. "Arrest him. He pushed me off the road and beat me up." He looked at his feet. "And he stole my boots, too!"

"Papers!" the sergeant shouted. "And you, you with the lip! Get that Honda off the road. Somebody will smash into it. Push it over here and stay near it."

"I left my papers at home," Taro said.

The sergeant walked back to the cruiser and sat behind the wheel. He spoke into his microphone, looking out of the window to read the Suzuki's characters and numbers. Taro glared at Saito and Saito studied a raspberry bush next to the wheel of the Honda.

"Right," the sergeant said. "Thank you."

He jumped out of the car and walked over to Taro. "Forgot your papers, eh? You're a liar and a thief, boy. And under arrest." He turned and faced Saito while the constables handcuffed Taro and led him to the back of the cruiser.

"You. Tell your story. What happened here?"

Saito swallowed. "I was riding up this road and saw the Suzuki slipping around. He'd taken the curve too fast and must have hit some loose gravel. He fell and I stopped to see if I could help. He was just lying there and I thought he might get run over, so I dragged him into the weeds."

The sergeant narrowed his eyes. Saito bowed. "That's the truth, Sergeant."

"And the boots?"

Saito looked down. "They are mine. His shoes are there," he persisted, "must have come off as he fell, I suppose."

"Yes?" the sergeant said. "How come that fellow says you forced him off the road and then beat him up? You were fighting. Shifty Eyes! You may as well admit it—look at that lip!"

"I've had this lip all day, Sergeant. A bug must have bitten me this morning."

"Come here," the sergeant said. He looked at Saito's lip. "Yes, I can see the bite, in the corner here. A deerfly. O.K., that much is true then. But you're lying too."

One of the constables returned. "Saito's papers are in order, Sergeant. The fools were probably playing chicken, and the moron on the Suzuki lost. He should be grateful he's still alive."

Taro's head appeared at the cruiser's window. "I'll remember your face, you bastard! When I see you again I'll—" He spat.

"You'll what?" the sergeant asked.

"I'll kill him!"

"Good idea," the sergeant said. "If you vermin would kill each other off we wouldn't have to work so hard." He turned to Saito. "On your way! And don't let me see you again today or I'll run you in. We'll think of the charge later. Harassing a deerfly or something like that."

Washino-san gasped when she opened the door.

"It's me, Miss. The police inspector you saw this morning. I came to return your grandfather's boots. Here you are."

She took the boots and put them down carefully. "Thank you, sir. My, you look terrible! What happened? Where are your shoes?"

"I lost them, Miss. It doesn't matter, they were old."

"Oh, *no*! Do come in, please. You can't go home in your socks."

He turned and walked to the gate. The sharp gravel hurt his feet but he tried to walk normally. He opened the gate, turned, smiled at the gaping girl, turned again, and walked off. His lip was worse; he could feel it throb. He found the Honda and tried to kick the starter, but it snapped back and hit his unprotected foot. He hopped about on one leg, made a full circle, and tried again. The engine caught.

"Samurai, hah!" he muttered as the Honda hobbled slowly over the lane's badly paved surface. He reached a main thoroughfare and turned the throttle. The engine coughed, failed, coughed again, and died. He braked. He was out of gas. He peered hopefully inside the tank. Nothing. He shook the motorcycle. Still nothing. He felt very tired. He had no idea where the nearest gas station could be. He would have to inquire. The closest house was the Washino cottage. He parked the Honda and began to walk back. His foot hit a sharp stone. The pain was so intense he had to lean against a tree.

"Samurai," he mumbled again. Noble warriors in lacquered armor, in feathered helmets, armed with long curved swords. To imitate the ancients is a foolish game. Prince Ch'ieh, ha! Kwannon, ha! The name of the goddess infuriated him most. Now he knew why she smiled. Because fools like himself hurt their toes, and ran out of gas, and were insulted by baboons in uniform. No wonder Kwannon was amused. He limped on.

"You're back," Washino said. "Oh, I am *so* pleased."

"I ran out of gas, Miss. Can you tell me where the nearest pump is?"

"Surely. But please come in. You must have a bath. The tub is full. And have some sake. My grandfather has gone to sleep already, with his boots next to the bed. He was so pleased. After the bath you can taste my noodle soup and some fried shrimps. *Do* come in."

When Saito sat in the wooden tub a few minutes later and felt his fatigue evaporate with the steam, he laughed for the first time that day. The swelling in his lip was going down and it no longer hurt. He sighed with joy and reached for the sake jug perched on the edge of the tub. He refilled his cup and sipped. He could hear Washino-san busy in the kitchen on the other side of the thin wall. The spluttering would be the shrimps falling into hot oil, being fried in a delicious layer of crackly batter. The spluttering stopped. The door of the bathroom opened an inch. Two large slanting eyes peeped through the steam.

"Is the water hot enough, Inspector-san?"

"Yes, very nice."

"Enough sake?"

"Oh, yes."

"After dinner I want to hear everything that happened. Fortunately, this is my night off from my job. You can stay as long as you like."

Saito waved the steam away. "Until tomorrow morning?"

"Is the story that long?"

He tried to think of a suitable answer.

Washino giggled. The door shut slowly.

Saito folded his hands and bowed. He hoped that Kwannon hadn't heard him. He hadn't really intended to insult her. It was only because he had hurt his toe. Surely the goddess would understand.

▧▧ 3 ▧▧

SAITO'S SUMMARY

CHIEF INSPECTOR IKEMIYA SAT BACK AND ALLOWED HIS right hand to caress the shadow of a bamboo leaf, silhouetted sharply on the empty center of his desk in one of the largest rooms of the forbidding building that housed Kyoto Police Headquarters. The shadow seemed to feel the touch of his fingers, veered away, and came sliding back again.

"Amazing," Ikemiya said. "You're an unusual young fellow, Saito. Now let's go through the case again. I've read your report but I always prefer my inspectors to inform me in their own words. Let's start from the beginning—and take your time."

Inspector Saito cleared his throat and studied the small bamboo bush growing from a glass jar on the windowsill. "Yes, sir. Let me see now, it all started when I bought a bowl of soup from Mrs. Taiko's son."

The chief inspector nodded helpfully. "Yes? Go on."

Inspector Saito took courage. He was still young,

twenty-six, and he hadn't been an inspector for long. The presence of the portly officer reclining in the leather-upholstered chair at the other side of the desk unnerved him, but he plunged ahead bravely.

"A week ago Tuesday, sir, at three o'clock in the afternoon, I was walking through the city and passed the high school south of the silver pagoda. Young Taiko was there with his cart, selling soup which he ladled from a big pot. The pot is heated by a hibachi. He's there every working day, and I had eaten his soup before—noodle soup. So I stopped, chatted with the young fellow, ate the soup, returned the bowl, paid, and walked on. I didn't know his name but I liked the fellow—he's easy to talk to. He isn't very bright but he makes a living and he's always cheerful.

"I was just about to cross the next street when a squad car came racing along and stopped next to Taiko's cart, some five hundred feet away from me. I turned and began walking back to see what the constables were up to. I didn't want to run, however, and by the time I reached the cart again it was all over. I saw them push Taiko away from the cart, lift the pot of soup and the hibachi, take something out from underneath—something small—and handcuff Taiko. They took him away with them, rather roughly, leaving the cart unattended. As it represents a certain value, I asked some boys from the high school to take it into their compound and make sure nothing happened to it. Then I came back here."

The chief inspector offered Saito a cigarette. "Very well. And then? You didn't take action right away?"

"No, sir. It wasn't my business. I am with the homicide branch and surely the constables knew what they were doing. I had guessed by then that they had found drugs in the cart. But somehow I couldn't forget the incident and as the principal of that high school is an acquaintance I went to visit him. According to the director, Taiko-san has been selling his noodle soup opposite the school ground for at least a year. He is popular with the boys and also with the school's staff. There is no drug problem at that particular school. My uncle didn't think Taiko-san had been peddling junk."

"And then you checked with the seventh precinct."

"Yes, sir. I remembered the number on the squad car and traced it to the seventh precinct. One of my classmates from the Police Academy is an inspector there. I went to see him. My friend told me that Taiko-san was still under arrest, that a small quantity of heroin wrapped in plastic had been found in his cart, and that Taiko-san insisted he had no idea how the heroin got there."

The chief inspector's dark eyes glinted behind his heavy spectacles. "Yes—now we get to the interesting part of your summary. Let's have it."

Saito stubbed out his cigarette. He looked neat and efficient in his dark suit, white shirt, and narrow tie.

"Quite, sir. I asked my colleague how the constables knew the drug was hidden under the hibachi. He told me that the boy's mother, Mrs. Taiko, had come to see him. She told him her son had been selling drugs to the kids for some time. She said she had warned him many times, pleaded with him to change his ways, and done everything she could, but the insolent punk had just laughed at her. She didn't want to denounce her own son, but she had to consider all the other mothers of the kids at the high school. She couldn't allow innocent youngsters to become corrupted, to become slaves of horrible drugs."

"How did she know her son was a dealer?"

"She said he had been spending a lot of money lately and had even bought a car, an impossibility considering the small profits of his trade. She had become suspicious and had gone through his belongings and found a supply of heroin hidden in his room. Then she had spied on him and discovered the secret compartment under the hibachi in his cart."

"Very well. What did you do then, Saito?"

"I went home and thought, sir. What bothered me was that the heroin was found under the hibachi in the cart. Taiko's hibachi is a clumsy metal container filled with burning charcoal. I couldn't understand that he would have picked such an impractical hiding place. It meant that every time he made a sale, the pot of soup would have to be lifted out of the cart and the hibachi taken out as well. I've read reports on the methods of street dealers. They usually revert to all sorts of tricks, like taking the money from their customers first and delivering later. It's usually done in a roundabout way, so that no contact between dealer and customer can be proved. They will hide the junk in a garbage can, for instance, or under a loose brick. They certainly don't lift hot pots and hibachis and then replace them again, all in full view of anybody who happens to be around."

"True."

Saito coughed. "Yes, sir, but thoughts aren't much by themselves. I asked permission to see Taiko-san and my colleague took me to his cell. We questioned the suspect at length. He continued to deny the charge. He isn't a very intelligent young man but he appears to be sincere. He's a pleasant, ordinary sort of fellow, sir."

"Did you tell him his own mother had accused him?"

"No, sir. But I did ask him about his mother and he

had nothing to say about her. He was more responsive
when I asked him about his father. Taiko Senior sells
vegetables in the northern street market. Young Taiko is
the couple's only child. He seemed fond of his father and
very disappointed that the old man hadn't come to see
him."

"Is the father fond of his son?"

"Yes, sir. I went to see Taiko Senior at his market stall
and he almost broke into tears when I mentioned his son's
name. He said he hadn't gone to the police station because
he couldn't bear to see his son a prisoner. He also said
he couldn't believe his son would peddle drugs."

"Did the father confirm that his son had been spending
a lot of money lately?"

"I asked about that. Apparently young Taiko has bought
a car, a secondhand one. I found out where he bought it.
The car was purchased on time payments with a ten per-
cent deposit."

"Right. Then what did you do?"

Saito sighed. "Then—well, then the unpleasant part
of the investigation started. I never like having to become
personal, but—"

The chief inspector smiled sadly. "But that's what we
have to do. Pour some tea. You must be getting a dry
throat."

Saito got up and poured two cups from an antique brass
kettle resting on an ornamental hotplate on the side of
the chief inspector's desk. They raised the cups, bowed
slightly at each other, and sipped the hot bitter brew ceremoniously.

Saito put his cup down. "Thank you, sir. I went to the
house of the Taiko family. It is a small wooden house in
a row in the northern quarter. Lower middle class, neat,

well kept. I found the neighborhood store and pretended I was looking for the Taiko house. I said that I was a real estate salesman, that the Taikos were interested in buying a larger house, and that I wanted to make some inquiries. The young lady in the store was very helpful."

The chief inspector grunted. Saito wasn't a particularly handsome man, but he did have a way with the ladies— his boyish charm, no doubt. "Go on."

"Yes, sir. The young lady in the store told me that old Taiko is fairly well-to-do and that he is a nice man, most regular in his habits. Young Taiko is his only child. But the Mrs. Taiko who made the complaint isn't his mother. She is the young fellow's aunt and his stepmother. His own mother died."

"Aha! And how did she die?"

"An accident, sir. About a year ago the two sisters went boating on Lake Biwa. It was autumn then, just like now, when the leaves show the delicate colors of the season."

"Go on. I am familiar with autumn and the leaves."

"Sorry, sir. The sisters went to see the maples on the lake's shore. There was a sudden gust of wind, the canoe capsized, and the younger sister drowned. The older sister, the present Mrs. Taiko, was found clinging to the overturned canoe."

"Right. That was a year ago. What did the coroner say?"

"Accidental death, sir. Mr. Taiko was very upset, of course, and the older sister took over the household and comforted him. Some four months later he repaid her for her services by marrying her. She is a few years older than he is and not very attractive."

"Could the younger sister swim?"

"No, sir."

"Can the older swim?"

"She said she could not, but I went into the matter and have been able to prove that she can. There are some statements to that effect attached to my report, sir. Friends and acquaintances say that she can swim, and very well, in fact."

The chief inspector pushed himself free of the desk, scratched his chin, and grinned. "You can bring in your famous book now, Saito. I'm ready for its venerable instruction. I've heard you are very fond of it."

"It was part of my studies at the academy, sir, and the thesis I wrote on its significance helped me pass my final exams."

"I had to study it too, Saito, but I've never used it. I always considered it to be an interesting antique."

Saito inhaled sharply. "Oh, no, sir. It's very up-to-date."

The chief inspector laughed. "Very. *Parallel Cases Under the Pear Tree*, a thirteenth-century manual of jurisprudence and detection. Absolutely the latest thing. Let's hear the relevant passage."

Saito opened his briefcase and took out a book wrapped in a piece of brocade. He unfolded the cloth with deft movements.

"Very well, sir. The fourteenth arrest, section B. *'A man and his wife accused their son of unfilial behavior. The judge berated the son in front of his parents; drawing his sword, he ordered the parents to kill the son. The father wept and said he could not kill his son. The mother reviled the lad, took the sword, and attacked him. The judge stopped her and subsequently questioned her relationship to the young man. It turned out that she was the son's stepmother. The judge thereupon put an arrow on his bow and shot her dead. This gladdened the hearts of all who heard about it.'"*

The chief inspector got up and walked around his desk. He stooped and read through the text. "Yes. That was during the later Chin Dynasty, near the year 1000, if I remember correctly. You have delved deeply, Inspector, but times have changed. I am relieved to note that you haven't shot Mrs. Taiko through the head with your pistol. I don't think such a drastic deed would have gladdened my heart." He went back to his chair. "Well, let's have the end of it."

"Yes, sir. You see, I just couldn't accept that a mother would accuse her own son. And I certainly couldn't believe that a mother would set her son up. If he were found guilty he would be out of the way for many years. Now why would a mother want her son out of the way?"

"Why?"

"Because he was interfering with her peace of mind, sir. Young Taiko believed that his aunt had killed his mother. He was suspicious of her, and probably had voiced his suspicions at one time."

"So you assume."

"Yes, sir. There is another relevant case in the same section of the *Pear Tree* book. I won't read it to you, but it has to do with a mother who accused her son of a crime so that he would be put to death by the officers of the court. In this case the mother was having illicit relations with a monk. She tried to remove her son to cover up her own crime."

"So?"

"We need proof these days, sir. The Chinese magistrates of a thousand years ago had more freedom."

"A dangerous situation, Saito, that has since been changed."

"Indeed, sir. What I did was somewhat unorthodox. I asked my assistant, Sergeant Kobori, to accompany me, and together we invited Mrs. Taiko to come with us. We didn't tell her where we were going."

"You didn't order her to come with you, I hope?"

"No, sir, we were polite, but she did come. We went to the lake and hired a canoe, the very same canoe she had used when she went boating with her unfortunate sister last year. I researched that little outing and was able to pick the same date. We went out on the water. That was yesterday, sir—rather a misty day. Every now and then we floated through a fog bank. Two of my constables were close by in another boat, pretending to be fishing. When I signaled them they launched a piece of plastic foam, more or less in the shape of a body, wrapped in a gray kimono with a pattern of roses. Mrs. Taiko's sister had been wearing such a kimono on the day of her death. The constables did their job well. They had even attached some water weeds to the object. It came drifting toward us just as we entered another patch of fog."

The chief inspector was staring at the inspector.

"Then Mrs. Taiko screamed, sir, and tried to jump out of the canoe. Sergeant Kobori grabbed her just in time or we would have capsized. She was in a bad state, nearly fainting. But she made a full statement later. She had hit her sister with a paddle and then pushed her overboard. She also admitted she had placed the heroin in her stepson's cart. She had bought the drug in the Willow Quarter out of her savings. We have meanwhile arrested the dealer—he was rather a stubborn suspect, but he did in the end confirm what Mrs. Taiko said. He says he sold her the heroin as medicine, because she was supposedly suffering from diarrhea."

"Good," the chief inspector said. "But we may not be able to obtain a conviction on the murder charge. The coroner's report did mention a hemorrhage on the first Mrs. Taiko's temple and there are photographs of the wound. But to claim that the paddle inflicted the wound may be tricky. Your suspect's confession gives a wealth of detail, and she also states that she planned the foul deed, but she may go free if some clever lawyer makes her retract the statement."

Saito had risen and was standing at attention, the briefcase containing the slim volume of ancient wisdom clasped under his left arm. "I don't think so, sir. The reconstructed scene on the lake touched her subconscious. She wants to be punished now, to be given the opportunity to wipe out her bad karma."

"Very well, Saito."

The chief inspector stared at the door that Saito closed behind him with a discreet and gentle click. He shook his head. "Clever," the chief inspector muttered, "*too* clever. We'll have to keep him in hand."

4

SAITO AND THE SHOGUN

"LET'S HAVE ALL THAT AGAIN, SERGEANT," INSPECTOR
Saito said and offered a cigarette to dilute the sternness
of his order. They were standing on a narrow country
road just south of Kyoto, the great and teeming temple
city of Japan. The sergeant, a middle-aged man, neat in
his army-like uniform, faced him, and a younger constable
stood respectfully to the rear.

The sergeant pointed. "Over there, sir. A small three-
wheel truck, parked under the trees near the river, almost
out of sight from the road."

The inspector peered. He saw the canvas hood. "Yes."

"It was found by a fisherman, sir, about an hour ago.
He went away but I have his name and address. He didn't
see the corpse under the truck but he thought something
was wrong. The doors of the truck were open and several
empty crates were shattered near the vehicle. The driver
was missing, of course. The fisherman telephoned our
station from the big house over there on the hilltop, Sakai-

san's house. Me and the constable came over and investigated and found the corpse. We know the victim—young Muto. Muto lived close by, on a small farm on the other side of the village proper. He raised livestock and sold it in the Kyoto street market. The crates must have contained chickens, for we found their feathers. As we ascertained that Muto was murdered, we radioed for assistance from the city police—and you came, sir."

Saito looked at the sun rising above the mountains. He had been ready to go home after an uneventful night behind his desk at Kyoto Headquarters when a girl from the radio room brought him the message. The message mentioned a truck and an accident but wasn't too clear and, as he knew that country policemen tend to exaggerate, he had decided to come out by himself and check the case before bothering the experts.

"Let's have a look," he said.

"He's not a pretty sight, sir."

The sergeant was right. Saito saw a gaping wound on the back of the skull, and fat flies feeding greedily on the clotted blood. He sighed, walked back to his car, unclipped the microphone from the dashboard, and activated his radio.

The experts took their time and gave him a chance to investigate a little further by striking up casual conversation with the local policemen. The sergeant didn't say much, reserving his energy for puffing the cheap Shinsei cigarettes that Saito kept handing out, but the constable, a man of Saito's own age—on the short side of thirty— talked easily.

"A robbery?" Saito asked. "Taking a human life just to get a few chickens?"

"The thief may have been surprised, sir. Perhaps Muto had gone into the bushes to relieve himself and the thief tried to get the chickens, and Muto came barging back and surprised the thief. The thief panicked and killed Muto."

"By hitting him on the *back* of the head?"

The constable nodded thoughtfully. "True, sir. It doesn't sound likely, does it? Maybe the thief found Muto already dead and took the chickens afterward."

"Yes. Maybe he didn't even see Muto's corpse. You said you found him under the truck."

The sergeant grunted.

"You don't think so, Sergeant?" Saito asked him.

The sergeant kicked a pebble.

"So who steals chickens around here?" Saito continued. "This is fairly sparsely populated country. You two must know everybody in the area." Saito stared at the sergeant.

The sergeant cleared his throat. "There's a man on the other side of the river, sir, a man by the name of Mishi. He is a widower and he has some small children. He used to be a professional wrestler. Mishi is fat, so fat that he cannot work and has been declared an invalid. He collects welfare but the money isn't enough. Mishi likes to fish. It's about the only thing he can do, because he doesn't have to move about when he sits in his boat—and he has strong arms, so he can row. He has several boats and his kids use them too. The kids are troublesome—they sneak about and steal."

"With the father's consent?"

"Yes, sir," said the sergeant.

The constable dropped the stub of his cigarette and stood on it. "Yes. But Mishi hasn't had much luck. Wrestlers have to be fat, but when they grow older the fat gets in their way and they have to retire—and everybody forgets them. Mishi never got into the big money. His savings dwindled away when his wife kept on having kids. Then she died—she was blown to bits when Mishi's house exploded last year."

"Exploded?" Saito pushed himself free from the hood of his car. "How do you mean, *exploded*? Houses don't explode, do they?"

"Mishi's house did."

"How did that happen?"

"Nobody knows," the sergeant said gruffly.

The constable frowned.

"Is that so, Constable?" Saito asked.

"Everybody knows, sir."

The sergeant almost snarled. He turned toward the constable and took a deep breath, but Saito stepped between the two men and smiled pleasantly. "This is very interesting, Sergeant. Please tell me more about the explosion."

The sergeant glared at the constable, who was polishing a dull spot on his boot with his handkerchief.

"Well?"

The sergeant sighed. "The constable is right, sir. Maybe I should tell you, but it won't do any good. It'll do bad. As you said, this is the country—everybody knows everybody. People talk, but only to each other. You're an outsider, sir. If I talk you may investigate further—you'll make out all right, but I may lose my job."

"I'm a policeman too, Sergeant."

The sergeant studied Saito's stylish dark suit, the white shirt, and the narrow black tie.

Saito touched the sergeant's shoulder. "Go on, Sergeant. Don't worry. I've never gotten a colleague into trouble yet."

The sergeant cleared his throat again, very thoroughly this time. "Yes, sir. Mishi's house blew up because his wife slipped a piece of birch into the stove. It had been filled with gunpowder. So we think, sir."

"And how did the gunpowder get into the piece of birch?"

"Mishi's kids had been stealing firewood for a long time, sir, and people were getting tired of the thefts."

"What *people*, Sergeant?"

The constable stopped polishing his boot. His lips moved. "Sa—"

"No!" the sergeant barked. "Don't mention names, Constable. That's an order!"

The constable laughed. "The sergeant is a bit nervous today, sir. I think you should be told what we know. This village is a mess, and the mess is all one man's fault. If we don't denounce him we'll all continue to live in hell. We may have to go to hell anyway, sir, but later on— there's no need to live in it now."

Saito studied the constable. The man had a sharp but open face. "So? Who is the criminal?"

The constable pointed at the house sprawling on the hilltop. "Sakai. Who else? The mountain-ogre who has us all by the tail and pulls us the wrong way. I can't prove that Sakai made the wooden bomb, but it's just the sort of thing he would do. He's a bad man, sir—he's grown rich in bad ways, and he won't share his wealth. What does it matter to him if Mishi's kids steal a few of his birch logs? The Mishi family needs wood to keep their bodies from freezing, while Sakai burns wood for the orchids in his greenhouse."

"Shut up," the sergeant growled, and came to attention.

A new Datsun convertible had stopped behind the two police cars and a squat old man with a shaven skull was trying to extricate himself from the low driver's seat. The sergeant ran to the car and extended a helpful hand.

"Never mind," said the old man. "I'm not a cripple. What do we have here? Trouble?"

"Yes, Sakai-san," said the sergeant, "trouble. Young Muto got himself killed. His head is bashed in, sir—we found his body under his truck. Somebody tried to hide the corpse. And his chickens have been stolen. This is Inspector Saito from the Kyoto police, Homicide Department. There are more police officers on the way."

Sakai had managed to get himself out of the Datsun and began to walk in the direction indicated by the sergeant.

"Hold it," Saito said quietly. "You can't go in there."

Sakai proved himself capable of quick movement. He whirled around and glared at the inspector. "You're telling me where I can go and where I can't go?"

"Exactly. Don't go in there."

Saito was lighting a cigarette. He kept his voice low and steady. Sakai took one more step and stopped. The constable was in his way, his legs apart, his hands folded at his back.

"Are you on guard here?" Sakai asked.

"Yes," the constable said loudly. "You heard what the inspector said—you can't go in there."

Saito ambled up. "We don't want to disturb the area. I'm waiting for my colleagues. Do you know the victim, Sakai-san?"

"Of course. I know everybody around here. What's this about some chickens?"

"We think there were chickens in Muto's truck, but they aren't here now. Somebody may have stolen them."

Sakai laughed, in a deep hoarse voice, as if he had gravel in his throat and chest. "If anything is stolen we don't have far to look. Did you tell the inspector about our charming Mishi family, Sergeant?"

"Yes, Sakai-san."

"Well? What are you waiting for? Get in your car, drive across the bridge, and check Mishi's yard. You'll find Muto's chickens."

"Mishi has chickens of his own, Sakai-san. How do I know which are his and which were Muto's?"

Sakai repeated his mirthless laugh. "Do I have to teach you your business? Mishi feeds his fowl on anything he happens to have around. Muto fed his chickens on good corn—I know because he bought his corn from me. If Mishi doesn't own up to his crime he'll soon give in if he sees you begin to cut the chickens' crops. Just one crop filled with corn will hang him. I've told you many a time you should take care of Mishi and his brood. This is what we get when the police are too soft on thieves. If you had listened to me—"

"Let's go, Constable," the sergeant said, bowing to Sakai. He turned to Saito. "We'll be back soon, sir. The bridge is only a mile from here, just beyond the river's bend."

"Stay here, Sergeant."

The sergeant was halfway to the patrol car when he hesitated. Saito's order had been formulated gently, but there was authority in his soft voice.

The sergeant came back. The constable hadn't moved.

Sakai snorted and was ready to regain the initiative when two black Toyotas arrived and six men spilled but. They were greeted by the inspector.

The sergeant sidled up to Sakai. "I'm sorry, Sakai-san, but I have to obey these officers. I will go to Mishi's place as soon as I can."

Saito strolled over. "Ah, Sakai-san. I don't think you can be of use to us now but I'll come to see you later. Go home and wait for me."

Sakai's reply was both furious and surprised. "You mean you're telling *me* what to do? I'm on my way to the city. If you wish to see me you can come tonight—or tomorrow, if I decide to spend the night in Kyoto."

"Not tonight. I'll probably be over at your house around lunchtime. Sergeant, come with me. Constable, direct Sakai-san. His car is wedged in between the others, but if you help he can get out. If not, you can ask my colleagues to back up a bit."

Saito walked to the truck, followed by the sergeant. The constable positioned himself in the road. Sakai breathed deeply. The constable had taken out his nightstick and was twirling it around.

The experts busied themselves and left, taking the corpse with them.

The constable shook his head. "They didn't find much, did they?"

"No—but we know a little more. Some of the fingerprints on the doors and the crates were made by children. And poor Muto got his head bashed in by his own wrench, while he was standing up. So the kids didn't kill him. Now we can make sure that the thieves were the Mishi kids. Go to the Mishi house, Sergeant, and do exactly what Sakai told you to do—then come back and report to me."

"Here, sir?"

"No, the constable can show me a restaurant—I wouldn't mind a bit of breakfast. Don't be too hard on Mishi, Sergeant. The days are gone when a judge would be interested in the theft of a few birds."

"Shall I mention the murder, sir?"

"Mention it, yes. If he becomes nervous—guiltily nervous, I mean—come and call me; we may have to bring him in for questioning. I leave that to your discretion, Sergeant. You have a way with people, I can see that—I don't have to tell you what to do."

"Thank you, sir."

The sergeant left, smiling. Saito was smiling, too. So was the constable. "He does get upset easily, sir, but he means well—it's just that he's so frightened of Sakai."

Saito and the constable sat at a table on a balcony overlooking the river. The restaurant owner had been serving them personally. Saito watched the constable pick his teeth contentedly. He smiled. "My favorite dish too, Constable—fried river crab and pickled radish. That was the best breakfast I've had in a long time. You chaps in the country don't know how lucky you are. Look at this view! All I can see from my office is a blank wall."

The constable nodded. "That may be, but I would still prefer the city. This place has been getting on my nerves. It's beautiful but it's so small—small-minded, I mean, sir."

The owner brought a pot of tea and poured two cups. Saito raised his and bowed slightly. The constable bowed back and they drank the tea ceremoniously, holding the cups with both hands.

Saito replaced his cup with a little click. "Tell me what

you think happened. You know, don't you? You've been acting very sure of yourself. Tell me why. Who is this bad guy you mentioned?"

The constable grinned. "Sakai, sir. Sakai killed young Muto. I'll tell you what I think—even if the sergeant is right and it'll be the end of me here. What I'm going to tell you may be useless, because the way the people are here, we'll never be able to prove anything."

"Go on."

"Sakai is a powerful man, sir, and an evil man. He was a lieutenant in the secret police during the war. He tortured people, and killed them once they told him what they knew. I've met ex-soldiers who served in the same area, in Java. Even our own army was afraid of Sakai. When the war was over, the Americans were looking for him, but he managed to escape."

Saito frowned. "A lieutenant in the Kempeitai, eh?"

"Yes, sir. The Kempeitai ceased to exist, of course—but after the war Sakai settled here. He had some gold that he used to buy land. The people didn't want to sell, but he forced them. He's good at manipulation and he can always get help. He's the richest man of the entire district here now—he even owns the stores in the village, and the mayor is Sakai's right hand. He exercises the same kind of authority as the shoguns did in the old days. But his rule is always for selfishness and evil, never for good. Nobody dares to oppose him, except Mishi's kids—and Muto."

"Are you from here, Constable?"

"Yes, sir. My father lost his land to Sakai and died of grief. My mother moved in with relatives."

"I see. What did Muto do to provoke Sakai's wrath?"

"He slept with Sakai's mistress. Sakai's wife was sent

away when she lost her teeth. This girl comes from a rich sex club Sakai used to go to. He must be boring company, or she wouldn't have smiled at Muto."

"Wasn't Muto discreet?"

"Very. He only saw the girl when he was sure Sakai was in the city. But somebody must have breathed a word into the old boy's ear."

The constable handled his cup and Saito poured more tea for both of them. They drank in silence.

"So Sakai planned to kill Muto and Muto didn't even know he was in danger," Saito said. "That would explain why he wasn't on the defensive when Sakai met him. You think Muto was set up this morning in that out-of-the-way spot?"

"No, sir. Sakai planned to kill Muto, yes, but their actual encounter today was by chance. I've been watching Sakai for years and I know how his mind works. He uses fate. How can I explain his method? Do you know what I mean, sir?"

"I think so. You mean that Sakai doesn't act until circumstances turn his way?"

The constable slapped his thigh. "Exactly. Sakai is a true evil spirit who, as the priest says, moves with the currents of heaven. Sakai knew that he would get his perfect chance if waited and stayed alert. I'm almost sure that Sakai went out for a walk today at dawn. He's always complaining that he can't sleep and has too much energy. His land borders the road and he must have seen Muto drive his truck into the bushes. Sakai strolled up, they talked for a minute, Sakai pointed at something, Muto turned—"

"Yes?"

"But somebody saw Sakai cross the road. Today is

market day. A lot of the local farmers were up and about, driving into town with their vegetables. But they'll never say anything."

"That's right," the sergeant said. He had stepped onto the balcony from the shadow of the restaurant. "You're a fool," he continued in a whisper. "The restaurant owner is just inside with his ears perked. He'll be on the telephone in a minute and Sakai will crush us like cockroaches. Sakai's friends run the city like he runs the village. Your eagerness has ruined all three of us."

"Sit down, Sergeant," Saito said. "You're just in time for breakfast. How did your investigation go?" He waved to the owner who was, indeed, hovering behind the sliding doors.

"Thank you, sir, I'm not hungry."

"Of course you are. One more plate of the same, my friend, and another pot of tea," Saito ordered. "Now, Sergeant, tell me what you found in the chickens' crops."

"Like Sakai-san said, sir, I opened two of them and the second was full of corn, so Mishi confessed that his kids had stolen the chickens."

"Had the kids seen Sakai?"

"They saw him walk away, but they didn't see him kill Muto, and they didn't see the corpse either. It's a rather low truck, and the kids were in a hurry, as you can imagine."

"Good!" the constable shouted. "We have witnesses!"

The sergeant squealed with rage. "Idiot! The kids are eight and ten years old, and known thieves! Who will believe them?"

Saito pushed the sergeant back into his seat. "Calm down. We've had enough of your antics. The constable says there will have been other witnesses—farmers who saw Sakai go into or come out of the bushes. And there's also Sakai's girl friend. She knew he wasn't in the house during the time of the murder, and he may have bragged about it to her when he came back."

The sergeant shrugged. "An ex-whore, an unfaithful mistress. Nobody will believe her either."

"I disagree. I think we have enough to make a move. When you've finished those tasty crabs we'll go to the Sakai mansion and arrest our suspect. Once he's no longer free and capable of hurting them, the witnesses will come forward. We'll also accuse him of filling a log with gunpowder with the deliberate intent to blow up poor Mishi's house—and Mrs. Mishi's death turns that caper into manslaughter. We'll delve into his past and charge him with any crime that crop's up. Once a tyrant sits in a cell, he becomes a mangy dog."

The sergeant poked at his crabs with a chopstick.

"You're still not convinced, Sergeant?"

"No, sir," he said gloomily. "The case will be thrown out."

Saito smiled. "You're a country cop. I'm a city cop. Homicide cases never get thrown out of court, because the press makes a living out of them. I know every journalist in Kyoto. If we hurry, Sakai's arrest will be in the evening papers. Eat your crabs—you're delaying justice."

The constable sat next to Saito as they drove to the hill.

"Sir?" he ventured.

"Yes?"

"How come I could convince you so easily? I'm from here and I know what I'm talking about—there was no doubt in my mind. But why did you believe me? It's only my word against his."

"Two reasons, Constable. I've dealt with criminals and Sakai made a nasty impression on me when he arrived on the scene. A squinty, blown-up, poisonous toad if ever I saw one. But that was only an impression."

"And the other reason, sir?"

Saito stopped the car and asked the sergeant to hand him his briefcase from the back seat. "This book, Constable, *Parallel Cases Under the Pear Tree*, a thirteenth-century manual of jurisprudence and detection. An antique book, Constable, containing cases solved by truly brilliant Chinese magistrates. There are fools who say the book is out of date, but there are still wise men in the police academies who advise their students to learn from the past. But brilliant detection can be used both ways. The Kempeitai studied the ancient wisdom too." He flipped through the book and smiled. "Here we are—Case 18A— let me read it to you.

"'*When magistrate Fu of the Sung dynasty*—' fifth century, Constable '—*was magistrate of Shan-yin*—' a Chinese province, as you know '—*two men got involved in a dispute about the ownership of chickens. Fu asked, "What do you feed the chickens?" One man said beans, the other said rice. Fu had one chicken killed and its crop cut; it contained beans. He thereupon fined the man who fed rice to his chickens.*'

"You see? Sakai probably learned the book by heart, just as I did when I was a student. This morning, when the fisherman used Sakai's telephone to call you, Sakai knew that you would find the corpse within the next few minutes and worked out his defense. He tried to defend himself by attacking you—the police authorities, of all people—for not dealing with a minor theft, while you were still investigating a murder. By suggesting a solution to the question of who stole the miserable chickens, he hoped to involve his other enemies. Muto was already dead, but he still wanted to get rid of Mishi and his kids. He surmised that you would charge Mishi with the murder—or the kids. But that would be the same thing since the kids are minors and their father is responsible for their behavior. It was a clever trap, but the fool forgot one basic rule. When a bystander in the case of a crime suggests a solution, he immediately becomes a suspect himself.

"And there was something else I'm sure you noticed. This is a small village, and everybody knows everybody. Muto had been buying Sakai's corn. Yet Sakai never expressed the slightest concern for the victim. Maybe that's natural in a tyrant and an egotist who has had his way for many years, but it doesn't make a very good impression on the officers of the law. It makes them think, doesn't it?"

Saito turned around. The sergeant seemed a different man—he was almost smiling. Saito laughed.

"Won't Sakai look silly when you and the constable arrest him!"

"I hope you'll witness the arrest, sir."

"But of course—thank you for the invitation. This is your case and will bring you much credit, but I'll be honored if you will let me follow its various stages. It'll be good to see you put the handcuffs on the villain and drag him to the car. Be sure to drive him slowly through Main Street so that the villagers can see the mountain-ogre in his true form. Then they'll know that the divine power the emperor himself has invested in you will crush this little fellow and make him do proper penance for his vile deeds."

The sergeant lowered his eyebrows and made an attempt to tighten his facial muscles. He almost succeeded in looking ferocious.

"Right," Saito said, "let's go."

The sergeant hesitated. "You say you will be with me on this case, sir?"

Saito straightened up behind the wheel. "You have my solemn promise, Sergeant, and I swear by the blood of the samurai that's in my veins." The sun broke through a cloud and the inspector's head was clearly outlined against a bundle of fierce light that suddenly filled the small car. The sergeant bowed his head briefly. The constable grinned.

Saito started the Datsun's engine and pressed a button on the dashboard. A siren hidden behind the car's grille whined ominously and a blue revolving light popped up and flashed from the roof. "Here we go," Saito yelled, and squealed the car's tires through a curve. He turned the wheel again and the Datsun shot up Sakai's driveway.

Sakai tumbled out of his front door as the car slammed to a halt. "What the hell ... ?"

The sergeant jumped out. "Come here, Sakai."

Sakai's round bald head seemed ready to burst. He yelled an obscenity and was ready to add another when the sergeant's hand hit his cheek with full force. Sakai staggered back, tumbling into the constable, who grabbed his arms, twisted them back, and applied handcuffs.

"You're under arrest," shouted the sergeant. "You're suspected of murder."

Saito stepped forward. "That's correct." He whispered

into the sergeant's ear. The sergeant nodded. His fist hit Sakai's chest. "You, take off your shoes."

Sakai didn't hear what he was told. His face was even redder than before and his eyes bulged. The constable stepped around him and pulled out his nightstick. "Take off your shoes, right now."

"What's all this?" a soft voice asked.

A young woman had stepped out on the porch and the policemen nodded at her. The woman was attractive and well dressed in a purple kimono printed with a pleasing design of roses. She looked at Saito. "Why is the master taking off his shoes?"

The sergeant spoke before Saito had finished his smile. "He is suspected of murder, Miss, and prints were found near the body. The ground was muddy, so we need his shoes."

The woman looked at Sakai. "But you've just changed your shoes, haven't you?"

Sakai's flabby mouth gaped for a moment. The constable's nightstick hit him viciously on the leg. Sakai squealed with pain.

"Where are the shoes he was wearing when he came back from his walk this morning, Miss?"

The woman smiled at the inspector, then turned to snarl at her lover. "Oh, so dirty, I had to push them into the septic tank, with a stick. And first you made me lift the lid by myself." She rubbed her back. Her eyes rested coldly on Sakai's face. "Didn't the doctor tell you that I'm not strong?"

Sakai moved toward the woman. The constable's stick hit Sakai's leg again. "Stay where you are. I'll get the shoes, Sergeant. Show the way, Miss, please."

Sakai tried to step back into his shoes but the sergeant

pushed him back to the porch and forced him to sit down. He bent down and tore off Sakai's socks. The constable came back, holding up a plastic bag. "Got them. Disgusting evidence but just what the judge wants to see."

Saito stepped up to the sergeant. "Why don't you take the car and drive the prisoner to your jail? The constable and I will talk to the lady here and ask her to sign a statement." He had spoken loudly and the woman bowed. "I will do so with pleasure, sir. I have much to tell."

Sakai opened his mouth and the constable lifted his stick. Sakai's curse changed into a groan.

"I don't need the car," the sergeant said. "Thank you, sir, but the prisoner and I will walk. Do you have some rope, Miss?"

The woman brought several yards of strong twine and the sergeant knotted one end to the chain connecting Sakai's handcuffs, admired his handiwork, and jumped back. The suddenly tightened rope yanked Sakai to his feet. The sergeant turned and walked away, his prisoner following painfully, hurting his bare feet on the pebbles of the driveway. The woman's teeth showed as she watched Sakai stagger down the hill.

"There goes the master," the constable said. "You don't seem to mind, Miss."

Saito caught her as she swayed. "It's all right, Miss, please go inside." She leaned into his arm.

"He killed Muto," she whispered hoarsely.

"Did he tell you?"

"Yes, but I know much more."

She signed her statement an hour later and the constable shook his head as he reread it to himself. "There's almost too much here, sir. If we can find further witnesses Sakai will go to jail for the duration of the universe."

The sergeant had come back.

"Tell us what happened," Saito said.

"I had a hard time, sir, dragging the prisoner to jail. He didn't follow easily and I had to pull quite a bit."

"Did the people see him?" the constable asked.

The sergeant nodded grimly. "They attacked him too, and I couldn't defend him very well."

"Nothing serious happened, I suppose?"

"No, sir, he's just a bit bruised. They really hate him out there."

The constable sighed happily. "It's almost too good to be true."

Saito rose and thanked the woman. He stood briefly at attention while he faced the sergeant. "Congratulations on a splendid job. May I suggest that I accompany you to your station to take down the villagers' statements? It appears that the suspect faces a multitude of charges and I have some experience in phrasing reports."

The sergeant leaned against a doorpost; the constable jumped up and bowed to Saito. "Be our guest, sir."

They worked until late in the night, piling up statements, signed by the villagers, who had been waiting impatiently outside the station and were ushered in one by one by the constable.

"Thank you, sir," the sergeant said as Saito made ready to leave.

The constable handed Saito the phone.

"Saito?" a gruff voice asked.

"Yes, Chief Inspector-san."

"What's keeping you?"

"I volunteered a little assistance, sir. The sergeant and constable here managed to arrest a tricky murderer and

I helped with the paperwork. I'll be on my way back in a minute, sir."

"Gadding about in the country," Ikemiya said sadly. His voice hardened. "Hurry back."

Saito smiled at the phone before putting it back gingerly. As he drove his car out on the main street the villagers were lined up on the sidewalks, bowing their thanks.

"That's what happened to magistrate Fu of the Sung Dynasty," Saito mumbled as the car picked up speed. "And when he came back to the capital the emperor made him a prince. All I can expect is some witty criticism and a kick back to my desk." He was still mumbling as the Datsun joined the heavy traffic on a speedway leading into Kyoto. "Ikemiya is right, *Parallel Cases Under the Pear Tree* is not the right book to study anymore. Times have indeed changed."

⦚⦚⦚⦚ 5 ⫻⫻⫻

SAITO AND THE SACRED STICK

"YOU LOOK TIRED," CHIEF INSPECTOR IKEMIYA SAID. "I think you should take off for a couple of weeks."

Saito nodded while he thought of objections. The recently solved murder case hadn't involved all that much effort. Why should he be tired? Besides, a healthy young police officer shouldn't be suffering from strain.

"Right now, Ikemiya-san?"

"Right now."

Saito got up and bowed. But of course, if the honorable chief deigned to give an order . . . "Thank you very much."

Ikemiya looked grim. "Don't bother to thank me. I'm trying to prevent all of you going to the beach at once. That's what you guys did to me last year and it left me with a bunch of morons that didn't know the difference between first- and second-degree murder."

"I'm sorry, sir."

The chief inspector cheered up considerably. "Stay

away for two weeks and I'll make sure you get another week during the summer."

"Many thanks, Ikemiya-san." The door clicked behind the inspector. The chief grinned and tried not to listen to his own thoughts. That Saito! A sly fellow under all those good manners. Hard to find fault with but who wants to face perfection? Ikemiya grunted pleasurably; it would be a nice break not to have to deal with his brilliant assistant for a while.

The subject of these reflections, suddenly faced with the emptiness of having nothing to do, felt pleased too. He realized, while marching briskly through the corridor, that he didn't really care much for work. Two weeks of free space, a pause in time—his reasoning almost gave way to meditation. Was this perhaps an opportunity to return, as the Buddha suggested, to the source of non-doing? He shrugged the profound thought away; he was an ordinary man, with a hole filled with emptiness ahead, and the hole would have to be plugged.

He marched on, to his room and his telephone, and dialed.

"Oba-san?"

"Yes?"

"Saito here. I would like to spend two weeks in Suyama, starting tonight. Would you please ask Uncle if that's all right?"

The answer was positive and Saito was on his way. He caught the bus a few hours later, dozed off and woke up again, to admire a layered landscape of rice fields against a backdrop of mountains reminiscent of antique Chinese scroll paintings. The bustle within the great city of Kyoto behind him was already forgotten and his mind reached forward, visualizing rustic scenes.

Uncle Saito had lived in Suyama for many years now and the inspector was used to spending his holidays in the old man's house. Uncle had never married and was looked after by elderly Mrs. Oba, who replaced female company of a different order. The present simple house also contrasted with Uncle's previous lifestyle, for apart from being a scholar he had also been a mighty businessman once, until a misfiring investment burned up his resources and forced him to retire on less than a tenth of his original wealth. The event had transformed him into a semi-hermit, smiling about the foolishness that proved nine-tenths of his energy uselessly spent. "Gadding about madly," he would tell his nephew, "got me away from the core, until my karma kindly changed and made me find here what I insisted on missing for so long."

The inspector nearly fell asleep again but the bus driver applied his brakes before swerving the vehicle into the next steep curve. He could see the ocean far below and remembered the spot, for it was here he had come out of his shock, five years ago. His parents were dead then, suddenly killed in a car crash, and Uncle had picked him up, to change his mental environment. He had phoned the old man he hardly knew and blurted out his report of the calamity.

"They're dead, both of them, I'm alone."

"Not quite," Uncle replied, "I'm on my way."

Uncle appeared.

"They're gone, Uncle, the car slipped off a cliff."

"The bodies?"

"The undertaker picked them up."

Uncle bowed deeply to pay his respects to the departed. Then he smiled. "We must have tea."

Saito made the tea, after spilling hot water and breaking

a cup. Uncle waited patiently; a small old man in a threadbare kimono, but emitting much strength, then, later during the funeral, and again in Suyama.

Much had changed for young Saito although he continued to live in his parents' house. He was well-off financially because his father was a surgeon and his mother an M.D., and both had had flourishing practices. There was insurance money as well and the inheritance of his grandfather, an aristocrat who served as a vice-admiral with the Imperial Navy during World War II. Young Saito continued his studies for another two years, then switched over to the Police Academy, and Uncle, although never over-enthusiastic, stayed interested in his nephew's career. He even showed up for the graduation ceremony to sit in the front row between two grizzled commissioners and didn't seem displeased when his nephew's teachers stepped forward to declare that they had never had a student as diligent and intelligent as Saito Masanobu.

The bus wound down a narrow road and the sloping roof of Suyama's Buddhist temple became visible. It was surrounded by gnarled pine trees perched on cliffs sprayed by incoming waves. Saito saw Uncle's little house on the edge of the town. He mused about the old man's life again. Uncle had been a man of many talents, an originator, among others, of the Japanese electronics industry—not quite his field as his first Ph.D. was in philosophy; his essays on Kant and Hegel were still in print and part of current examination material.

The inspector remembered how he had asked Uncle for advice a few times, and how the old man invariably managed to change the subject. Even so, Uncle's haphazard and even frivolous commentaries always proved worth listening to.

"Shall I join the police, Uncle, or rather go for a degree?"

They had been walking in a park, following the shoreline of an ornamental lake. "Look," Uncle said, "there is a carp over there, a fat fellow with wavy fins. Just now I saw a pike dashing along and there are small fish about too, playing between the rocks. The pike likes to hunt but the carp prefers to overeat, and the little fish usually get caught. There's a lot of variety wherever you look."

"What's the best kind of fish, Uncle?"

"To eat? Well, that depends. A matter of taste I would say, but they're all good at the right time. Last week Mrs. Oba prepared a sole, French style, with nuts and so forth, not bad at all when the fancy takes you. Sometimes I prefer fried smelt, though. Ten sen a pound smelt used to be when I was a kid, but even with today's money smelt is not dear."

"Shall I become a police inspector, Uncle?"

"Why don't you find out what it is you cannot refrain from doing and then push straight ahead?"

Saito grinned as he got ready to leave his seat. Uncle's out-of-the-way wisdom was great, especially because he never moralized. Whatever his brand of Buddhism might be, it wasn't holy and there had been occasions, when young Saito was still a student, that Uncle would suddenly pop up in the city and invite his nephew for an outing into the Willow Quarter. Full of sake, and with his arm around a hostess, Uncle would expound complicated theories, only to lose track of what he was trying to explain and wander off, leaving the hostess to his nephew, claiming that it's good for the young to finish what the old have started.

The days that Uncle wanted to start something were over, however. Now he stayed at home, dividing his time in periods devoted to gardening, meditating, and napping, with a book in between. The books weren't new either. Uncle had studied them before and their contents now only appealed to his sense of humor, or relativity. "It's all so clear, Nephew, why did they ever bother to try and write it out? But I can't blame them, can I? I made the same mistake myself."

Uncle was approaching extreme old age and his heart malfunctioned. Each attack struck a little deeper. Oba-san, the housekeeper, had just turned sixty and still kept him going, in her subdued but vigorous manner.

The bus rumbled to a stop and Saito picked up his suitcase, containing two kimonos, some books, a recently purchased stock of expensive rice paper, three of the brushes that father liked to use, and an inkstone that once belonged to his mother. He planned to write an essay: *On the Motivation of the Intelligent Lawbreaker*. The purpose of the essay was twofold. He planned to have it published in the *Police Gazette* to increase his fame, and he wanted Chief Inspector Ikemiya to be annoyed by its depth in order to release his spite.

The bus had stopped and Saito walked through its narrow aisle. He smiled guiltily for he was aware of both aims. Fame was just another illusion of course, to tie him down, and spite was a negative emotion that would tie him down even further. Saito smiled as he hopped out of the bus. The essay might hang like a millstone around his neck one day, but he badly wanted to attack Ikemiya, by refuting the chief inspector's slogan, "Observe, conclude, solve, make an arrest," with the invariable postscript, "and spare me your cleverness, Inspector third class. We did not join the police to split hairs."

Oba-san pushed the sliding door open, knelt, and bowed

until her forehead touched the threshold of the small hall. Then she took off the inspector's shoes while conjugating a polite sentence, in both the "I" and the "we" form. She pulled the suitcase from his hand as he stepped on the worn but immaculately clean floormat.

"Good to see you, Oba-san." The exclamation came easily, even though Saito was slightly irritated with the old woman's servility. He reflected that he had never been able to penetrate her mind although he was supposed to know Oba-san well by now. What did he really know about her except that she was Uncle's faithful retainer? Some factual material rose to the surface of his mind. The woman was a war widow, so much he knew. Mr. Oba, rather an awkward young man to judge by the snapshot on his wife's private altar, was shot by a Chinese sniper in Manchuria, 1942. The unfortunate hero, holding a long rifle, bowlegged, and squinting into the sun from under his military hat, hadn't known his spouse longer than a few weeks—apparently not long enough to make her pregnant. The inspector wondered if the soldier had found his wife attractive; she certainly wasn't attractive now. He looked down at her small shape compassionately. However she had projected herself in her younger days, she was a pathetic little old woman now with her irregular crooked teeth, heavy-lidded small eyes, comical topknot, and bony limbs. But she was hardworking of course, and although she might not be a sparkling companion she was certainly an excellent cook. It was only a pity that she knew all the nine thousand polite expressions by heart and used her knowledge continuously.

"Did the honored inspector have a good journey in the tiresome bus?"

"Yes, thank you."

"I am so glad that the honored inspector wants to visit this"—she couldn't say the house was lowly because it belonged to the honored uncle of the honored inspector—"house again."

"Yes, yes."

"I do hope that the honored inspector will not find the upstairs room too confined for his august presence."

Saito walked on, while Mrs. Oba scurried after his tall shape. He nodded patiently at the flowing stream of lilted little words and knocked on the door of the garden room. He heard Uncle's grunt, pushed the door open, knelt, and bowed.

"Welcome," old Saito said.

Mrs. Oba's mutter had gotten into Saito's brain. "I'm glad you allowed me to come again, Uncle-san. I do hope that my untidy presence will not clutter up the house."

Uncle's eyebrows shot up. "The bus ride must have been rough; your mind seems to have shaken loose. This is your house too, why apologize when you make use of what is yours? Come closer and sit properly. The woman has gotten very stingy lately; I'm out of cigarettes again. Pass one over."

The inspector shuffled forward and crossed his legs. He pushed his present respectfully across the tatami and Uncle immediately tore the can open and shook out two cigarettes. He looked at the can's label while he smoked. "Ah, British." He coughed. "That's what I like, nothing but the best. If only I could convince that tightfisted old harpy..."

Saito smiled. He hadn't listened but admired the garden instead. It occurred to him that Uncle fitted in well with his surroundings. The garden covered little ground but its division in space, both horizontally and vertically, was perfect. Two artfully cut miniature pine trees represented a forest; a minute pond, locked in by lichen-covered rocks, was a lake; and the little hill that had been wheelbarrowed in but looked like it had bulged out of a vulcanic eruption was the mountain that ruled the landscape.

Old Saito, dressed in a faded, often-repaired robe, sat upright on a thin cushion. His black button-eyes glittered behind round glasses. Laugh wrinkles appeared around the corners of his eyes and thick, still sensuous lips. "You look fine, Nephew."

"So do you, Uncle. How is your health?"

"Bad, but I hardly notice. I still work in the garden but now I only clean what I can see from this room. Oba-san does the invisible part and even rakes the path these days. She claims that I can no longer bend my back easily. Nonsense, when I weed my back moves too. Besides, her raking is a poor excuse for doing a good job; you ever notice that women cannot draw straight lines?"

He raised his voice to reach Mrs. Oba, who had entered the room carrying a tray. The old woman giggled, knelt slowly, and pushed the tray between the two men.

"Only two cups? Aren't you joining us, woman?"

She took a third cup from her sleeve and placed it near the edge of the tray.

"Better. The inspector-san comes rarely and we have a hard time when we cannot benefit from his instruction."

Mrs. Oba agreed and made ready to phrase her assent but old Saito cut her short. When Mrs. Oba returned to the kitchen after the collective tea ceremony, Saito excused himself too and walked up the stairs to unpack his baggage.

The inspector was indeed at home and joined easily

into the harmony of the house. He ate with his uncle, made minimal conversation, and was called into the bathroom every night to massage the old man's back. He went to bed early and rose with the light, woken by the chanting in the garden room where Uncle sang Buddhist sutras, accompanying himself by hitting a fish-shaped wooden drum with a small stick. The monotonous drumming contrasted well with his quavering chant, exotic even to Saito's ears, for the old man didn't sing in Japanese, preferring the original old-Chinese text. "*Ha-ra-mi-ta shingyoóóóó,*" sang old Saito.

"What is that sutra about?" Saito asked during breakfast.

"About nothing at all," Uncle answered kindly.

"How do you mean?"

Uncle's chopstick pointed sternly. "Have another radish, she pickled them specially for you. I'm not supposed to touch them. They harm my stomach, she says."

Saito nibbled on the yellow slice of root. "Tasty. Is that sutra really about Nothing, Uncle? I have been trying to visualize total absence lately. It's the basic exercise of true Buddhism, is it not?"

"Any luck?" Uncle asked.

"Not really." Saito selected another pickled radish. "Or not at all, I should say. If I chase one thought away it is replaced by three others."

Uncle agreed. "But there are other exercises as well," he said, absentmindedly helping himself to the radishes. "To reach the source of the great mystery in the most direct manner may be well nigh impossible for a mind such as yours, but try something else." He chewed noisily. "Properly directed activity, for instance. The Buddha had a lot to say about that too."

"How does that go?" the inspector asked.

His uncle frowned. "You should know by now. Weren't you always the head of your class? Do everything well and don't worry about results."

Uncle shuffled off and Saito went upstairs. That evening the characters flowed easily from his brush and the essay filled page after page. The next morning he talked to his uncle again.

"What is a sutra, Uncle?"

"A string leading back to the source."

"And Nothing?"

"The source itself, where true insight lives in emptiness. Thoughts and concepts are always lies. Birth and death are no more than thoughts."

"My parents are dead."

"True, they're out of reach."

"You mean they're somewhere else?"

Old Saito puffed furiously on his cigarette. "Here, there, that's not at all what the sutra means. It goes deeper than that."

"I don't understand."

"Of course not. When you try to understand you automatically use your mind. What you need is the opposite instrument, no-mind, a useful tool that grows in quietness."

Uncle smoked peacefully. The inspector rested his eyes on the shades of green of moss and water plants. He remembered that his uncle had never comforted him by trying to explain suffering away, not even on the day of the accident that killed his parents. Yet Uncle's not-caring was not indifference but rather serenity; a helpful calmness that had put him at ease then, and now again when he listened to the old man's voice or his sutra chanting drifting into the upstairs room.

The holiday passed slowly and pleasantly. The inspector slept, ate, and calligraphed his essay. He went for walks about the small town and spent undisturbed hours on its majestic beach, and every morning he listened to the sutra.

Until, on the first morning of the second week, there was no chant. The inspector, freshly shaven and dressed in a clean kimono, waited in vain, kneeling and facing the window of his room. When he gave up and walked downstairs he found Uncle and Mrs. Oba at breakfast.

"Uncle, you didn't sing."

His uncle pointed at the altar in the garden room. "I couldn't. The stick is missing. Without the stick I can't hit the drum and I need rhythm to keep the words straight."

"The stick disappeared?"

"It did. Strange, don't you think? It's always there but it must suddenly have taken off. Sit down, Nephew, your food is getting cold. Oba-san cooked up a favorite of yours again. A pity you can't always be here; the food definitely improves when we have you around."

Mrs. Oba protested squeakily but the inspector didn't hear her. His eyes kept wandering toward the red lacquered altar table while he manipulated his chopsticks, grabbing the delicate little mushrooms floating in the clear bouillon that filled his bowl. How could the stick not be there? Could it have fallen on the tatami and been swept outside? But surely Uncle would have checked. Had anyone taken it? But for what reason? Together with the drum it might have some value but on its own it would be just another used spare part, valueless, antique or not.

The inspector put down his bowl and walked to the

rear of the room. Uncle waved him back. "Don't bother, I tell you it isn't there. Come back, or don't you like the soup?"

Saito sat down again and held up his bowl so that Mrs. Oba could refill it. He cleared his throat. "Could your stick be stolen?"

Uncle shook his head. "You're on the either/or again, aren't you, Nephew? If it wasn't mislaid, and it wasn't, because Mrs. Oba never mislays anything, and I, a helpless old man, wouldn't dare to do such a thing, then it must be stolen." A mushroom slipped from between his chopsticks. "There, helpless indeed, can't even hold on to my food anymore." He tried again, succeeded, and slurped the slippery object down noisily.

"So it must be stolen. Well, your logic seems irrefutable," the inspector mused. Mrs. Oba offered more soup. He shook his head.

Uncle laughed. "Don't be upset. A small stick leaves a small hole. Who needs to listen to my voice anyway? Especially at such an unearthly hour. I will change my devotions. Perhaps I'll just sit still instead and try not to fall asleep. The drumming always kept me awake." He felt his cleanshaven chin. "Yes. So shall I let you worry about the crime? You are a policeman after all and too much rest may dull your brain."

"I'll find the missing item," the inspector said and jumped up.

He left the room, but only long enough to wait for Mrs. Oba to go to the kitchen and Uncle to retire for his nap. When he left the garden room again he was sure that the stick wasn't there. He had also made sure that it wasn't outside the garden room because he had opened the doors and searched the area an energetic sweep of the broom might have covered.

The inspector went upstairs and tried to work on his essay. Adversity faced him. His brush wouldn't point, the ink didn't mix well, and his first character, thrown on a sheet of immaculate paper, was lopsided. He cursed, tried to regain his composure, lit and rubbed out a cigarette, and walked down the stairs.

He met Uncle in the corridor. Uncle smiled easily. He also met Mrs. Oba, ready to go shopping. Mrs. Oba dropped her bag.

The inspector left the house and aimed for the beach.

Long soft foaming waves rolled on until they touched his feet. A heron flew by, almost nipping the surf with its wings before soaring off toward a pale blue sky. It was high tide and he retraced his steps until he found a rock. He leaned against its warm side and lit a cigarette.

Crime in Suyama; a peaceful fishing village that attracts pleasant and usually older tourists during summer. The season was over now and the beach stretched on, almost surrealistically empty. Perhaps once in a while an unseemly event might take place in this environment but whatever the misdemeanor might be, it would have nothing to do with a quiet man enjoying his vacation. Yet here the inspector found himself, charged with tracing a sacred symbol.

He squatted and stared ahead. He saw his uncle shuffle into the garden room, pick up the drum and grasp vainly for the stick. He also saw him put the fish-shaped instrument back and return to the bedroom. Uncle would have been neither surprised nor upset. No stick, no sutra chanting. The harsh wind of bad luck could no longer sway

Uncle Saito; he would have been content to continue his contemplations.

The identity of the thief . . . into which group would the criminal fit? Any inhabitant of Suyama could be suspected, for the house, like most Japanese homes, was unlocked. Who would trouble himself to step into forbidden territory and grab a worthless object? Greed could clearly be ruled out. If not greed, then what?

He lit a second cigarette and contemplated the smoldering tobacco. There were only two possibilities: pure evil, the desire to make another suffer, or a more normal egocentricity; it could just be that someone was irritated by the ever recurring early morning chanting. The first theory made the inspector shiver. Would Uncle have an enemy who pursued him into his old age, who intended to destroy his beneficial ritual? But Uncle had retired a long time ago and no longer dealt with anyone except Mrs. Oba and his nephew.

The second possibility was more likely. Doing away with harassment. The police wouldn't prohibit anyone from chanting sutras, at any given time, so perhaps an atheist or a Buddhist-hater could have been tempted into breaking and entering, and theft. The inspector remembered a newspaper article mentioning an unknown person who had fired a rifle, aiming for the carillon in a Catholic church tower. A later article informed the reader that the suspect had been caught and that a psychiatrist had declared him insane. The sound of a carillon carries further than an old man's weak voice. In this case only the neighbors could be suspected.

He walked back slowly and found his uncle busy in his garden.

"Uncle?"

"Yes, Inspector-san. How is your inquiry progressing?"

"Uncle, do you have any enemies? Opponents of the past whose hatred reaches into the present?"

Old Saito stopped weeding and looked over his shoulder. "No, when I retired I said goodbye to my business acquaintances. Those who disliked me thought I had reaped well-earned bad karma. I was almost bankrupt, as you know, but I managed to pay my debts." He studied the blade of grass that he had pulled from the moss. "My moral debts as well."

"Did you have friends?"

"Friendship!" Uncle Saito pointed at a passing cloud. "There you have friendship, Nephew. The emotion is like a cloud: it forms, looks real for a while, and wafts away."

The inspector's inclined head acknowledged the statement, but Uncle had more to say. "Family ties are clouds too, Nephew. Is that all you came to ask?"

"Yes, Uncle."

"In which case I will continue weeding."

Saito went upstairs and stared out his window. The house was situated on the edge of the town. He could see only two others, one in the rear, the other to the side. The rest of the view consisted of fields planted with cabbage. He could talk to the neighbors. On his way down he met Mrs. Oba.

"Will the honored inspector be eating his lunch here?"

He said he would and noticed that her voice seemed squeakier than usual and that her eyelids drooped a little more.

"Your honored uncle tells this worthless person that you are conducting an inquiry."

"That's correct, Oba-san. Do you have any idea where the missing stick could be?"

"This witless old person will not be able to be of assistance."

He stopped on the porch. What could have moved Mrs. Oba to take the stick? Her strange behavior might be an indication of her guilt. Was he jumping to conclusions? Couldn't it equally well be that she was merely upset about the disturbance in the house? Why should a dedicated housekeeper wish to annoy her master? She was a devout woman too; surely her discipline would prevent sacrilege. Saito ruffled his short hair. His agile brain shot off on a tangent. Would she perhaps know who the suspect was and try to protect him?

The house in the rear of Uncle Saito's home belonged to an old gentleman who lived alone, squinting and stuttering. The neighbor introduced himself as a retired professor. The inspector said that he had bought a toy plane for the little son of a friend, that he had tried the model out and that it had disappeared over the neighbor's fence. Together with the professor he scrutinized the latter's garden. Meanwhile they talked. Did the professor happen to be a Buddhist too? And did he chant sutras just like the inspector's uncle?

The professor said that he adhered to the Buddhist faith but didn't partake in any of its ritual. "But I listen to your uncle's chant, every morning I do. He has a good voice, don't you think?"

"Certainly."

"Why didn't he chant this morning? He is not unwell, I hope? I always listen with attention, you know, it's a good start of my day."

A trail that led nowhere. The professor was a kind old soul, in spite of his squint and stutter.

Saito tried the other house. A maid led him to the living room where a portly middle-aged lady listened to the tale about his lost toy. She went with him into her garden. Mrs. Oba was beating a floormat next door.

"How the sound carries," Saito exclaimed. "Do you ever hear my uncle chanting sutras in the morning?"

"Oh, yes, he has such a dear voice, I think. But very often I don't hear him, as I come home late and it's hard for me to get up in the morning. I own a restaurant, you see, and we close after midnight."

"The restaurant facing the beach is yours?"

"Yes, I trust you eat there from time to time?"

"Not often," Saito said, "because I eat with my uncle but I do stop by for a jug of sake once in a while. You run a beautiful place, and the view is excellent from there."

She smiled. "When you come again please make yourself known. I will prepare one of my specialties." Her smile became romantic. "One of my waitresses comes from Kyoto. She is lonely, poor thing. She would love to talk with you."

Saito returned, mumbling to himself. A fat lady creeping into his uncle's house during the early hours, what a ridiculous idea.

During lunch he studied Mrs. Oba carefully. His observations led him to believe that the housekeeper was definitely under strain. But why, by the grace of all the Bodhisattvas, would this kindly woman wish to make life hard on her employer? Could it be that old Saito's sarcasm had hurt her deeply and that revenge was necessary to restore her peace of mind? It was true that Uncle did lash out now and then. Would one of his jokes have struck a nerve?

He felt his stomach cramp with fury and frustration and tried to correct his reaction. A detective is supposedly free of his case. He breathed deeply until the cramp subsided.

Old Saito coughed harshly.

"Are you feeling ill?" Saito asked when the attack wore off.

"A little perhaps. I think I'll lie down."

Mrs. Oba shuffled closer on her knees. "Shall I telephone the doctor?"

"No, just bring me some codeine syrup. That usually does the trick."

She stood over him while he swallowed his medicine, then made sure he went to bed.

The commotion lasted only a minute and Saito walked over to the kitchen to see if there was any tea left in the pot. Mrs. Oba poured. He put the empty cup into the sink. "What's Uncle's health like these days, Oba-san?"

Mrs. Oba had just lit a cigarette and looked at him guiltily. "I really stopped smoking so as not to tempt your uncle but sometimes I make a little mistake. His health isn't good, Saito-san. The doctor says that he won't survive his next heart attack. I do wish he was a little more careful. He shouldn't work in the garden at all anymore but he won't listen and he still wants to eat what he likes. You don't offer him any of the pickled radishes, do you, Inspector-san? It gives him heartburn on top of everything else."

"I don't," Saito said firmly.

When he looked into the bedroom later that afternoon his uncle was reading.

"I worry about your health, Uncle-san."

Old Saito put his book away. "Why? I'm dying slowly, you should know that by now. Death is the only certainty given in this life. It will all come to an end and I'm glad that I'm no exception. This badly functioning body is becoming too much of an unpleasant illusion, but it'll soon fall apart, thank heaven." He giggled. "You know what the doctor told me the other day? That I should be careful breaking wind because my intestines can no longer stand sudden differences in pressure. I ask you . . . but the young fellow is right, I'm sure. Perhaps there's some purpose to the last few years of life—it's not a bad idea to fit in previously obtained information—but we shouldn't exaggerate the worth of the final period. One of these days this person will be all done. Don't look so sad, Nephew, your own life is limited too. Think of that when you have a moment and reflect on how much you're trying to carry around. In that respect I've been lucky. I've lost much already and being released from carrying possessions has cheered my life appreciably." A thrush interrupted its flight to grab a twig of one of the miniature pine trees outside the window. Its joyful song penetrated the room.

The inspector ignored the bird. "When you die Oba-san will be alone. Have you thought of her? I don't think she has any money of her own."

"Not a single sen, and she isn't mentioned in my will. You're my only heir. The house isn't mortgaged and prices have gone up steeply lately. I also own the fields to the north, an acre or two, and I still have some bonds." He crumpled an empty cigarette pack. "Bah, out of tobacco again and she won't get me any more until the end of the week."

The inspector dropped his own pack next to the old man's pillow and left the room.

He found Mrs. Oba in the kitchen, scraping carrots.

"Oba-san, I've been thinking a little. Once Uncle goes you will be left without an income. As soon as I'm back in town I will see a notary and have him draw up a contract, specifying that you will receive a sizable sum monthly, sufficient to pay for board and lodging in whatever place you care to select."

She didn't look at him.

"I'm sorry, Oba-san. The subject is painful but I thought you should know that there's no need to worry about material matters."

He waited another moment.

"You heard me, Oba-san?"

"Yes. Yes, Inspector-san."

When he went to bed that night he was sure he would hear his uncle chant the sutra in the morning.

"Nephew," old Saito said during breakfast, "your inquiry does not seem to reach a happy end. I admit that I'm surprised. I can still see you after the final examination, when you received your commission. Several professors attested to your brilliancy and you proved them right because the newspapers mention your clever solutions from time to time. Wasn't there the case the other day where you traced a seemingly natural death to the deliberate faulty programing of a computer? And when you arrested the movie star's murderer not so long ago the journalists said that you had outwitted your quarry by thinking from an unusual angle. But when I ask you to retrieve a small stick you become confused and trip over your own questions."

"A little more patience, Uncle-san, please."

The inspector helped Mrs. Oba with the dishes. "I changed my plan, Oba-san. I do believe that I have misunderstood your desire. I think it would be better if I made sure that this house will be deeded to you, so that you can live here in peace, in an environment you are familiar with."

She dropped a rice bowl and he had to wait until she had scooped up the pieces.

"So I was thinking that it would be better to inform the notary that my uncle's possessions will pass to you. There'll be this house, some land, a few bonds, and whatever else Uncle leaves. Uncle has appointed me as his heir but I own too much already and if you would be here I could continue spending my vacations with you." He bowed. "If you don't mind, of course. I will telephone in advance."

Mrs. Oba was still sweeping the floor and didn't look up. The inspector left the house and marched gaily to the beach where he admired the graceful bodies of small sand birds racing along the tide lines. The sun had almost dropped into the sea and the elegant restaurant behind the beach was lit up by its orange rays. He went in, telephoned Mrs. Oba that he wouldn't be home for dinner, and asked to see the owner of the restaurant.

The portly lady came running from her kitchen. "Please come in, Saito-san, so pleased to see you." She waved a waitress down. "Etsuko, do you know who this gentleman is? That's right, the police inspector from Kyoto who I have been telling you about. You know, Saito-san, Etsuko has been with me for years but she is still homesick for the city. You know what, Etsuko dear? Take our honored guest to the table in the corner and keep him company with some sake while I cook up a lobster for the two of you. Do you like lobster *à la meunière*, Inspector-san? That's very good then, my fisherman brought in a beauty just now."

She bustled back to her stove and Saito followed the slender girl and enjoyed the liquor. The girl was both attractive and amenable to his low-key approach and when the portly lady served the lobster and saw how well the two were getting along, Etsuko was given the evening off. "A movie perhaps?" Saito suggested.

The movie, a lighthearted romance, proved to be just the right introduction for the rest of the evening, and night. Saito had set Etsuko's alarm clock for 6:00 A.M. and left before daybreak. When he checked the altar in the garden room he saw no stick next to the drum.

Uncle came out of the garden. "Come along, nephew, one of the rocks near my pond has slipped. You can adjust it for me."

When the rock was arranged old Saito admired his waterlilies before walking with the inspector again. "You go back to Kyoto tomorrow?"

"Yes, Uncle, but the sacred stick has not been found yet."

The little old man grinned. "No matter. It'll appear again, no doubt. I'm sorry I've been such a nuisance for you this time. We all have to make our decisions, and perhaps I expected the unreasonable."

The inspector bowed and left the garden by stepping over the side fence. He walked again to the beach, where he didn't see the surf, the heron, or the sand birds. His mind was made up now but not yet ready to order the decisive move and he smoked restlessly, leaning against his rock, lighting one cigarette with another. In the end he acknowledged the impossibility of sidestepping his conclusion, pushed himself off the rock and hurried back. He found Mrs. Oba in the bathroom, scrubbing the floor.

"When my uncle leaves us you'll have to join me in Kyoto, Oba-san. It's a pity that you will have to leave Suyama but I see no other possibility. I live in a large house and I'm quite alone. It is time that my life becomes properly arranged."

She tried to blow the hair away that hung over her eyes and straightened herself with difficulty. She blew her nose and rubbed at the tears that had almost crossed her cheekbones. She scraped her throat laboriously. "Very well, Inspector-san, when the time is there I will come to you."

"That's settled then, Oba-san." He touched her cheek lightly. "Please don't cry."

She blew into her handkerchief and began to mumble.

"What's that?"

"Please don't mention contracts and notaries again, Inspector-san. That is unnecessary. I serve the Saito family."

The clearly articulated syllables of the sutra tumbled brightly into the open upstairs window. It seemed as if old Saito's voice had grown overnight. The plock-plock of his hand drum made the entire house vibrate. The last words, *ma-ka-han-ya shin-gyóóóóó*, trembled under the low ceiling and mingled with the sound of the surf that was carried in by the sea breeze.

The inspector left after breakfast. His essay was by no means finished but he had read the thoughts of another and interpreted their meaning correctly.

"I'm sorry," Oba-san whispered as she accompanied the young man to the bus stop. "Your uncle said that I had to bury the stick in the garden. I didn't want to do it for it would interrupt his chanting but he said that the stick had to be hidden, as part of a puzzle he had thought up to test your insight."

They stood at the bus stop. Saito checked his time-table; there were still a few minutes. "So I must have disappointed him for I never found it."

"It didn't matter," the woman said shyly. "Last night he told me to bring it in again."

"Really?" Saito asked. "You know why he changed his mind?"

Oba-san giggled behind her hand. "It was such a strange day yesterday. After you talked to me I felt happy and I must have been singing in the kitchen, an old tune that my father taught me when I was little. I thought I had forgotten it but I suddenly knew the words again."

"Uncle heard you?"

"Yes. He told me to come into the garden room and I had to sing the tune for him again. After that he told me to fetch the stick and put it back on the altar."

"You told him that you will eventually join me in Kyoto?"

Her hand quickly covered her mouth again. "No, how could I remind him of his own coming death?"

The bus stopped.

He found a seat in the rear of the bus and looked back, waving at the rapidly diminishing figure, bowing and flut-tering a handkerchief.

||||| 6 |||||

SAITO AND THE FOX GIRL

THE GIRL WAS SAYING "GOOD MORNING" AND "PLEASE excuse me," but Inspector Saito didn't hear her. She had a low voice and the mopeds gurgling through faulty mufflers that were passing the fence at speed tore her melodious words to shreds. Besides, Saito was busy. He had spent the early morning cutting wood and was now stacking the neatly split birch logs in a shed close to the fence. The girl approached and studied the inspector, smiling at what she saw. Saito's virile body was clad only in a pair of tight jeans. Sweat gleamed on his bulging shoulder and chest muscles.

"Good morning, Saito-san."

The disturbing explosions of the last moped rattled away in the distance. He pushed up the strip of cotton that was bound around his hair to prevent perspiration from running into his eyes.

"What? Who are you? How long have you been here?"

106

She laughed. "I'm Hamada Yoshiko and I've been here only a minute. Please excuse me for disturbing you."

He bowed. "You're not disturbing me. Saito Masanobu at your service. Ha, I'm glad those bikes have gone! They're on their way to some contest, I'm sure. They always pass here on Sunday morning. They like to disturb the peace. What can I do for you, Hamada-san?" He glanced at his watch. "You're an early visitor indeed. I haven't even had breakfast yet."

He wondered if he should invite her into the house. The presence of his recently engaged housekeeper, Mrs. Oba, would prevent any accusation of being too fresh with a young lady. It had been different before the old woman began to work for him—inviting ladies into the privacy of his home had gotten him into all kinds of trouble. Either the guests were insulted by his hospitality or they would expect him to make a pass. Then, of course, if he did, there would be more trouble—telephone calls, letters, hysterical outbursts. Good old Mrs. Oba—not much to look at, bent over, the indifferent possessor of most irregular teeth, a somewhat bad-tempered ogre at times. He had inherited all her qualities, pro and con, when his uncle left her to him.

Mrs. Oba, housekeeper class-one, grade-A. He hardly recognized his house these days. She had repaired the torn paper in his sliding doors and windows, cleaned and aired every single straw mat, arranged fresh flowers under the scroll displaying his grandfather's calligraphy, and found everything that had been lost during the years he lived in the large house left to him after his parents died in a car crash. She had restored the very spirit of the place. There was also her excellent and subtle cooking. He was indeed looking forward to her breakfast now.

He glanced at the girl. He had no idea who she was, but she seemed respectable in an odd way. Her western clothes fitted her well. He admired the short jacket and the blouse holding a rather aggressive bosom. He especially liked her head, triangular under the long hair. Saito had never appreciated the traditional Japanese ideal of womanhood, prescribing thin faces, hardly any mouths, and elongated necks. This girl's mouth was full and moist under her prominent cheekbones and enormous, heavily slanted eyes. He thought he had seen her before. No, not her, but someone like her. Unable to grasp the image that floated through his mind Saito frowned furiously. There! the fox, of course, the *divine* fox. The complete image, so well known, fitted together quickly. He saw the small temple in the east of the city that he visited a few times a year, to admire the strange apparition enthroned in the rear of the quaint shrine—a female fox, twice life size, serene and upright, its eyes half closed in an inward smile, its supple chest adorned with a bright red bib.

"I'm sorry, Inspector-san," the girl said. "I know this isn't a good time to visit, but I didn't want to impose on you in your office and hoped you wouldn't mind . . ."

He dried his face with his handkerchief. "You have a problem?"

"Yes."

"Come into the house and tell me about it. We can have breakfast together. I'm sure my housekeeper has cooked enough for us all."

"Won't she be surprised if you bring an unknown woman into the house?"

Saito grinned. The girl smiled back. "It has happened before, has it? My cousin says that you're not married."

"Your cousin?"

"His name is Hamada too—he's a constable at your headquarters. I don't suppose you know him, but he knows you, and he says you're the most intelligent and active officer on the force."

Saito bowed. "Your relative must be mistaken. Mrs. Oba!"

The door behind the balcony moved aside. "Yes, Saito-san?"

"We have a guest, Mrs. Oba—Hamada Yoshiko-san. Would you entertain her for a moment while I wash up and change?"

Saito showered and abstractedly selected a thin cotton kimono, thinking about his visitor. Hamada-san would be intelligent, he decided, but not well educated. She would probably fit into the lower middle class and have no schooling beyond ground level. She spoke the singsong local dialect that most citizens lose during high school, but the way she formulated her words and bore herself and her strange fox-girl face intrigued him.

Mrs. Oba coughed behind the bathroom door. "Your slippers are in the corridor, Saito-san."

"Yes," he reassured her. "I'm coming."

When he entered the dining room he found the girl kneeling demurely behind the low table, her back straight, her hands folded in her lap. The display of filled red bowls pleased him. Mrs. Oba was putting up a neat show, another complete breakfast with many side dishes. He looked at the pickles, the little fried mushrooms, and the piece of grilled squid.

"There are eggs too, Saito-san, scrambled American way," she told him.

"Great!" he said.

Mrs. Oba bowed and left the room.

"You have a beautiful house," the girl said. "Doesn't your housekeeper eat with you?"

"No, she's old-fashioned. Please eat, and excuse a lone bachelor for his bad manners."

She made the correct denying reply and he answered with another polite statement. There was no need to broach the reason for her visit yet; she would tell him in due time.

When most of the dishes were empty the girl put down her chopsticks. "There's an unpleasant matter. Would you mind if I told you about it now?"

"Please go ahead."

"It's rather a long story."

"No matter." Inwardly, Saito was exasperated. He had planned his day. He wanted to repair his wheelbarrow, read in the garden, take his old motorbike out for a ride in the country; he hoped the story wouldn't be too long. What could it be anyway? Why was a decent young lady visiting an inspector of Kyoto's murder brigade on his day off?

"I was raped," Hamada-san whispered.

"Ah," Saito said sadly. "When?"

"Last night, in the Daimon-ji temple opposite my father's little store."

"Last night? Why didn't you go to the police straightaway? There's a station in that neighborhood. I know its commanding officer—he's a good man."

"I wanted to consider my situation first. You see, I

can't prove anything. There were witnesses but they all enjoyed the spectacle."

Saito sipped his tea and looked at the girl over the rim of his cup.

"The monks raped me—two of them. There are five monks in that temple. The other three stood around. Their teacher wasn't there—the abbot, I mean. One of the monks called me in. I've known him for several years and he's supposed to be a holy man so I didn't suspect anything. He said he wanted to show me something. But when I was inside he closed the gate and dragged me to one of the buildings. He had been drinking. I tried to pull free, but he forced me. I couldn't cry out, he had his hand over my mouth. Can I light a cigarette?"

Saito pushed his cigarettes across the table and struck a match. "You don't have to tell me the details."

She inhaled the smoke deeply. "There are no special details. He raped me, then one of the other monks did too. They were drunk and clumsy. I wasn't hurt. I'm not a virgin and I take the pill, so there will be no pregnancy. I didn't defend myself and I acted as if I didn't object too much. Their names are Han-san and Gi-san. Han-san is fat and Gi-san is very small. The other three stood around and watched. They wanted to have me too but I said I was in pain and wanted to go home. I told them I would come back some other evening."

Saito nodded. "Good. If you had resisted you might have been badly hurt. Are there any marks on your body?"

"I have some bruises on my thighs. I'll show them to you if you like."

Saito put his cup down with a little too much force. "No, but the doctor might be interested. I'll take you to Headquarters now."

"No. I don't want to make an official complaint. My name would be in the papers and my parents would be upset."

Saito poured more tea. "I see. I'm surprised that this happened in Daimon-ji—that temple has quite a tradition. Some of the really enlightened teachers we read about now were trained there. The monastery must be six hundred years old. I visited it the other day to see the famous rock garden."

The girl's smile was close to a snarl. "The monks hire professional help to take care of the grounds. I've never seen *them* do any work. They go around our neighborhood three times a week to beg and collect money and rice. Everybody gives to them in order to translate good deeds into good future karma. It's supposed to be an honor to be allowed to give to the clergy."

Mrs. Oba came in to clear the table.

Saito got up. "Oba-san, my guest and I will spend another few minutes on the balcony."

He felt better outside, sitting next to the girl, without the need to look into her luminous yellow eyes.

"I'm a Buddhist too, you know," he said. "My parents used to support the temple of this quarter. Now that they're dead, I've taken over the duty. I know the priests and their teacher, a truly holy man. I even know his teacher—my parents were his disciples. He's very old now and retired somewhere in the mountains. I'm sorry to hear about what happened to you. What do you want me to do?"

She shrugged. "I don't really know. Maybe the priests and monks you deal with are of another type, but the Daimon-ji are no good. I should have known. Their temple is so close to our house and store I can see what they do—which is nothing. They go out at night dressed in ordinary clothes and drink and play around with street girls. Their teacher is hardly ever there. He has a car. When he's at the monastery the monks serve him. He plays his flute in the rock garden sometimes. I don't think they ever meditate. I can see them go into the meditation building and they ring bells and clap clappers and then they go out again to play cards in their own quarters.

"They don't train at all. They just spend a few years in the temple to qualify for a higher rank and then they leave as soon as they can to become dignitaries in the country."

"Yes," Saito said. "That sort of thing can happen when rules are relaxed. And now you say they have committed a crime. But what can the police do if you refuse to make an official complaint?"

He lit another cigarette and puffed thoughtfully. What if the girl was lying or exaggerating? She might have some reason to want to place the monks in a bad light. Perhaps there was some trouble at her father's store, or perhaps she had fallen in love with a priest who didn't return her feelings.

"Are you engaged?" he asked her.

"No, I'm free."

Yet she was taking the pill. He knew Constable Hamada, an elderly, responsible man with some of the strange features the girl had herself—the triangular face, the large, luminous eyes. "Hamada-san, I fail to see what I can do."

Her voice was cold. "You're right. Maybe I made a mistake. I visited my cousin last night after it happened. He mentioned you and gave me your address. He said it wasn't right what the monks did and that they should be stopped somehow."

She started to get up, but his hand restrained her.

"There were no witnesses," he said. "Do you remember if there was anybody in the street when Han-san asked you to come inside? It was Han-san, wasn't it?"

"There was nobody in the street. Han-san asked me in. He's the head monk."

"Do you know if they have mistreated other girls too?"

"Yes. I saw my friend Eido-san this morning. We've known each other all our lives. Her father is the greengrocer next door. I told her what had happened and she said they mistreated her too, some weeks ago. She hasn't told anyone, for she is ashamed—she's a bit of a flirt and she had often joked with the monks."

"What about you?"

She smiled. "I like men, but I've never liked the monks. I kept away from them."

She really does look like a fox, Saito thought. She's lying on a branch now, warmed by the sun.

He got up.

"Thank you for coming to see me, Hamada-san."

She bowed when he opened the gate for her. "Will you do something, Inspector-san?"

"I will, but I don't know what yet. Maybe you'll hear from me, but don't be impatient. My effort may take a while."

"Thank you," she said and walked away.

He returned to the house, angry with himself for making a promise that he very likely couldn't keep. He wouldn't have reassured her if she hadn't somehow touched him with her weird eyes and her weird manner—the manner of some other order of being.

Mrs. Oba was waiting for him in the house.

"What did you think of our visitor, Oba-san?"

The old woman's cracked lips pursed. "Be careful, Inspector-san. I knew someone like her once, a long time ago, when I lived in my parents' village. That person wasn't like the other people. She lived apart and grew herbs and she left us at night to roam in the woods."

"She did?"

"Yes. And in the woods she wasn't a human being."

He tried to laugh. "What was she?"

"A fox, Inspector-san."

"Did you ever see her as a fox?"

Oba-san mumbled to herself and shuffled away.

He tried to forget the incident as he went through the routine of what should have been a relaxing day. Nothing worked out, however. He dropped a piece of firewood on his foot and later hurt his shin on another piece. The motorcycle didn't want to start smoothly, even after he installed new plugs. When the carburetor flooded, he gave up in disgust.

He sat on the balcony and tried to think. But all his brain would come up with was the idea of waiting for Han-san and his cronies in a back street and beating them up. Revenge, however, is not proper police procedure. The police maintain order and restore peace along time-tested rules, causing as little interference as possible. Citizens have to be protected against others as well as themselves. He spent an hour in thought, went into the house, changed into a fresh pair of jeans and a leather jacket, and returned to the garage. This time the old Honda started easily. He rode into the mountains north of the city and took narrow paths without following any particular route. His mind was empty now and he was content to accept whatever he encountered.

What he encountered was a cabin in a clearing.

He leaned the bike on its kickstand, realizing that this was the old Buddhist teacher's abode, and he had once been given directions to it.

"Ah," the old man said. "You came here to tell me a tale? I thought you would bring me a gift. Your parents used to bring me gifts. A nuisance, you know. I never needed much and all that stuff would clutter up my room. I would have to give it all away. Your parents were troublesome people, and now you bring me a troublesome tale."

He reached over and patted the breast pocket of Saito's jacket. "You have cigarettes. Give me one. Even though I'm forgotten I still smoke."

Saito gave him a cigarette and lit it for him. He coughed. "Pah! It's too strong!"

Saito took it from him and put it out.

"You think that girl spoke the truth?"

"I'm not sure, sir, but I rather think she did."

"A fox girl. So the foxes are still around too. They never did like the others to pull their tails. Well, out with it, Saito, what do you want?"

"Your advice, sir."

"Advice!" the old teacher grumbled. "Advice. If you weren't so busy, Honorable Detective-Inspector, and if you didn't allow yourself to be pulled this way and that like a Bunraku doll, you wouldn't be bothering an innocent hermit. Your parents used to have a nice altar room. Does it still exist?"

"Yes, sir."

"Maybe you should retire there once in a while and destroy the questions that hum about in your mind."

The old man asked for another cigarette and this time

Saito waited in silence until it was squashed in the dented tin can that served as an ashtray. Then he rose and asked permission to leave. The teacher waved the request aside.

"You can do as you please," he said, "come when you feel like it, leave when you have had enough. But there's something you can do. There's too much that still clings to me. In the cupboard over there you will find cameras I used to spend too much time with. Take them. The big one is accurate and the little one may come in handy. It's one of those newfangled machines that is so sensitive it doesn't requite a flashbulb. Take it all. Take everything. There should be some film, a tripod, developer, and a leather camera bag."

It took Saito a while to pack the items and the teacher spent the time reading a newspaper.

"The *Kyoto Times*, Saito. It doesn't say much but it says it to a lot of people."

"Yes, sir," Saito said. "Thank you."

He rode back down the mountain path slowly, the teacher's bag strapped to his back. By the time he reached the city he was smiling.

That same evening he knocked on Daimon-ji's main gate. Temple day, he said to himself. First the old shack on the hill and now this glorious example of ancient architecture. I might as well put on a robe myself and perform the holy rites, he thought.

He knocked again and prayed. "Buddha," Saito said, "you are an Indian and you died two thousand five hundred years ago. I'm a Japanese and I live today. They tell me that you taught the Right Way. I also try to walk the path. If you're not too busy and too alien you might send me some help—I would appreciate it."

"Yes?" A young monk appeared at the gate.

Saito bowed. "Honorable monk, I am a journalist. I work for the *Nippon Export Times*. My superiors have asked me to write an article on this splendid abode and take some photographs of your detached environment. Please allow this lowly person to enter." He had dressed himself for the occasion. He wore a three-piece summer suit and had puffed his hair with a dryer. A false moustache graced his upper lip.

The monk hesitated.

"I know," Saito said, and bowed even deeper, "that I'm causing you trouble, but I have brought you a small present to please your spirit." He held up a bottle of American whiskey, packed in a splendid multi-colored box. "Please bear in mind that my magazine is of vital import to our great nation. It encourages foreign trade and earns some of the money that is needed on all levels of our society."

The monk accepted the box. "One moment, please. I will consult with my superior."

He was back within moments and ushered Saito to the main building of the temple complex. The head monk, seated on a pile of ornamental cushions, his fat legs loosely folded, inclined his shaven skull.

"Welcome. My assistant, Gi-san, will show you around."

"Thank you, venerable sir," Saito said. "My directors asked me to attempt to repay your kindness. When I'm done, and when you and your colleagues have time, I would like to invite you for a meal in a restaurant of your choice. I have been provided with ample funds."

The shaven skull gleamed once more in the light of

ornamental candles. "We accept. Please return to this room at your convenience."

Saito, guided by the servile Gi-san, photographed several buildings. He took his time. Gi-san posed, sitting in meditation on a balcony. The other monks appeared and stood, with folded hands, against suitable backgrounds while Saito's camera clicked. Saito was also taken to the meditation temple where the monks, after arranging their robes, sat on cushions in a neat row next to the altar where thick incense sticks smoldered.

Gi-san hit a heavy copper bell and the rhythmic, delicate sounds floated out of the open windows to the busy world behind the high walls. Saito took some ten minutes to set up his camera and take light readings. When the monks finally climbed down, he noted that they seemed stiff and happy to move about again.

He addressed himself to one of them. "You must spend many hours in this place."

The monk grinned. "We should, but usually there's no time—there are so many other things to do."

"Do you think I could meet with your teacher? Perhaps he'd allow me to make his portrait."

The monk shook his head. "The abbot isn't in right now. He's also very busy and has to divide his time."

The head monk appeared. "Are you done, journalist-san?"

"Yes, I think so," Saito told him. "Thank you very much."

"Good, then we can go. Please excuse us while we change our clothes. It won't do if we show ourselves in a restaurant in our robes. The people do not like to see us enjoy ourselves, so we oblige by changing."

* * *

Five gentlemen dressed in suits, their shaven skulls hidden by caps, joined Saito a little later at a side gate. Han-san guided the company to a gaudy bar in a street at some distance from the temple. After a few drinks there, they were taken to a back room where an abundant meal was served by miniskirted waitresses. Rice wine flowed freely, more waitresses appeared, the door was locked, and a free-for-all ensued. Saito kept to the side, using the space to manipulate his small camera, hidden under a napkin. When he was out of film he partook in the general merriment and even sang, slurring his words and stumbling about. Several of the girls made advances, but Saito waved them back to the guests of honor.

He regretted having shot his film so quickly when he observed Han-san in a tender embrace with a plump girl, silhouetted against a lurid poster on the wall.

All good things coming to an end, several of the monks expressed a wish to go home. They were having trouble standing and it was three o'clock in the morning.

At Daimon-ji's gate Han-san discovered the loss of his key. Saito, being tall, was asked to stand against the wall so the monks could use his cupped hands as a step. Then they pulled Saito up after them, for both Han-san and Gi-san were still active and wanted their newfound friend to join them for a final drink in their quarters.

But when Saito scaled the wall he fell on the prostrate body of a monk. Bending down, he saw the monk was bleeding.

"He must have scratched himself as he fell," Han-san said. "He'll be all right in a while. Just leave him."

Saito ignored Han-san, picked the monk up, and carried him to the main building. He dumped him on a mattress and shone his torch on the wound. The scratch was fairly deep and Gi-san, under protest, supplied a first-aid box so that Saito could clean the cut and apply a bandage.

Han-san brought out the American whiskey and they retired to the meditation temple to drink it. Saito had an opportunity to reload his camera and he made more snapshots of the two monks displaying karate chops and throws with the altar as backdrop. When he left, Han-san was asleep, sprawled out on a mat. Gi-san took him to the main gate and unlocked it. "Thank you," he said. "Come again."

Saito stumbled out into the night. He found a taxi and was home within a quarter of an hour, where a clucking Mrs. Oba helped him out of his soiled clothes and held his elbow as he swayed to the bathroom. A cold shower and strong coffee sobered him somewhat and he busied himself with the developer, spilling some but managing to make a number of fairly clear prints. Then he sat down and wrote a short article, "*Monks at Work and Play—a Night in the Life of the Daimon-ji Priests.*" The article consisted of a series of understatements that referred to the photographs. He found a large envelope, inserted the photographs that he had dried above the gas stove, and asked Mrs. Oba to phone for a taxi. Half an hour later he was home again and fast asleep.

Ten hours later he was behind his desk at Headquarters, sipping bitter tea and trying to decide whether another aspirin would soothe or further aggravate his pitiful condition.

A soft knock on the door made him frown.

"Come in," he whispered.

A constable entered, carrying a newspaper on a tray.

"The *Kyoto Times*, sir—I thought you might be interested."

"Thank you. Put it on my desk, please."

"My name is Hamada, sir. I've already read the article on the second page. I found it of much interest. I—ah—thank you, sir."

"Hamada!" Saito groaned when the door closed noiselessly. As if he didn't know. The long triangular face, the luminous eyes. He glanced at the article. The photographs were good. Under the title appeared the phrase, "from one of our freelance newsmen."

The article was much discussed, and not only at police headquarters. Further articles appeared on subsequent days. The Buddhist authorities became active. A chief abbot in a brocade robe, his skull protected from the sun by an acolyte carrying an ornamental umbrella, appeared at Daimon-ji's gate. His assistants, during a brief ceremony, accompanied the temple's teacher and his five disciples to their quarters, where they had to take off their robes. The robes were confiscated and the six men were sent away. Daimon-ji's gates were locked and sealed.

Other chief abbots came from other cities and decided that the temple should not be reopened for several years and should not even be maintained during that time. A spokesman for the sect to which the temple belonged apologized publicly in an open letter to the *Kyoto Times* and later on television.

When the weekend came, Saito slept late. He woke when he heard voices downstairs. Curious to see who was visiting Mrs. Oba, he got up and peeked through the window. The girl was on her way out of the garden.

When Oba-san brought him his coffee she gave him a

small parcel. She waited for him to open it. He fumbled to undo the minute knot and folded back the paper. The parcel contained a delicate wooden box. He lifted the lid. The small head of a fox carved out of mahogany stared at him with incandescent yellow eyes. He thought for a moment that the eyes were small jewels, topaz perhaps.

"Too expensive," Saito grumbled. "I can't accept such a valuable gift, Oba-san. It will have to be returned." But then he saw that the eyes were mere beads and that the sun shining into the box had created the illusion.

"I'm sorry," Mrs. Oba said softly. "I was wrong about that girl."

"She isn't a witch after all, Oba-san?"

"That doesn't matter," Oba-san said as she shuffled out of the room. "When I warned you last Sunday I showed my ignorance. Please excuse me."

"Yes, dear. I'll be down shortly for breakfast. Will there be any mushrooms?"

"Yes, and scrambled eggs."

Saito lifted the fox head out of the box and dangled it from its thin chain. Then he slipped the chain around his neck.

IIII 7 IIII

SAITO'S SMALL OVERSIGHT

INSPECTOR SAITO LOOKED AT THE SHORT, BROAD-shouldered laborer with some surprise.

"Did you commit a murder?"

"No, Saito-san, I didn't say that. I said that I smashed that fellow Takegaki's head with a crowbar."

The laborer spoke the singsong Kyoto dialect contentedly, rubbing his calloused hands. "But that's not the point. Takegaki has been dead a long time. He's been buried in concrete for twelve years. He's outdated, so to speak."

The precise characters in which the Japanese Book of Criminal Law is printed appeared as if on a small screen in the inspector's head. *Article 23: Manslaughter—the statute of limitations is twelve years.* He put up his hand. "One moment, Masao-san. Would you mind describing how the death of—what was your victim's name again? Takegaki?—of Takegaki-san took place?"

Masao leaned forward on the plastic chair opposite

Saito's small desk. He smiled helpfully. "That Takegaki wasn't in the boss's regular employ. We were building a factory and that fellow was making fun of me. The night before I had been partying with some of the boys—we got some girls, but the girls wanted nothing to do with me. They all wanted to do something with Takegaki. He was a smart sort of fellow with grease on his hair and a little moustache and a leather jacket. The girls like that sort of thing. Me, they sometimes call me Frog because I'm wide all over and I have this round head. When my buddies call me that I just laugh, but I could never take it from Takegaki. Follow?"

Saito nodded. "Yes, go on."

"So we were at the building site and Takegaki was imitating me, hopping around, croaking like a frog, and suddenly I grabbed that crowbar. With me swinging it, I thought he would shut up, but he just went on hopping and croaking. 'Let's see what you're going to do to me, Frog,' he said. 'See if you dare.' Well, that was *it*."

"You hit him?" Saito asked.

"Right. On the head. Just once, but his brains were all over. There was a water pump nearby with plenty of pressure and I cleaned up nicely afterward."

"And the body?"

Masao grinned widely. "What do you think? I was in luck. We had been pouring concrete so all I had to do was dump him into it, push a little, and tamp the surface down neatly."

Inspector Saito sighed. Confessions were often based on complete nonsense. He hadn't trusted this one when the sergeant phoned him from the hall desk at police headquarters. "Funny business, Inspector-san. A man says he killed somebody and is complaining about blackmail. Could you take care of it?"

As the youngest inspector of the murder squad, Saito often functioned as a garbage can. Perhaps he only had to listen to what his visitor wanted to say and somehow calm him and send him home.

Once they'd talked, however, he could see it wouldn't be that easy. Masao didn't seem to be overly intelligent but could easily be classified as an "honest skilled laborer." He wasn't hysterical or a neurotic intellectual type. If he claimed to have brained somebody twelve years ago he might very well have done so.

An outdated manslaughter, thought Saito. How do I handle this? He took out his notebook. "Where can we find the corpse, Masao-san?"

"Suido 1-chome, 2, Bunkyo-ku," said Masao. "I'm working in the same area again and pass the address every day in the bus. It's a nice building—we did a good job. Some company is manufacturing plastic eyeglass-cases there now. It won't be easy to break that floor. You'll need some heavy equipment, and even with pneumatic drills it will take a little while."

"What floor?"

"Second, in the rear," Masao said. "I can show you the exact spot."

"Why don't you just describe it to me?" said Saito.

"Go in through the front door at the top of the stairs, then walk straight ahead until you can't go any further, and turn left. He's about a foot from the corner in the rear wall. Don't drill deeper than two inches or you'll hit him. He should be just about the way he was when I put him there—they say concrete preserves well. Even his moustache should be in perfect shape."

A muscle in Saito's cheek moved. "Weren't the victim's relatives concerned about his whereabouts?"

Masao offered him a cigarette. Saito refused but flicked his lighter. Masao sucked in smoke. "No, he had no family at all. I was in luck there too. And nobody knew he was working that day because he kept to his own schedule. When he never showed up again the boys wondered what had happened to him, but I played dumb."

"On the day that you, uh, beat him to death," Saito asked, "didn't anyone see him come in?"

"No—with the exception of my buddy, Togawa, that is."

Saito wrote down the name and drew a neat line under it. Very nice. A little firmness wouldn't hurt. He would have to write a report containing some facts, at least. "Very well. And Togawa never said a word?"

Masao pursed his thick lips. "No, but he did talk to me. That's why I'm here."

Saito nodded. This would be the blackmail part. The case was shaping up. "Go on, Masao-san."

"Listen, Inspector-san. Togawa was my mate, right? We had been working together for quite a while. We always got on well together, maybe because we were different. He read a bit, and he had ideas—he still has ideas. He wanted to work for himself and after a while he did. He has a business in metal now—tubes and stuff, secondhand material. Sometimes it's lifted, but I don't care about that. If he wants to buy stuff that's found somewhere, that's up to him. But I *do* care if he comes to me to collect rent for twelve years. You follow?"

"Collect rent?" Saito asked.

"Yeah. I pay enough rent and now I can't even get married because Togawa gets half my wages—after taxes, not before taxes—which is good for him, because if he wanted that much I would have brained *him* too. He's clever. He doesn't take more than he can."

"Blackmail complaint," Saito wrote on a clean page of his notebook. He had also written down the date of the crime, February 28, twelve years ago. One outdated manslaughter and one workable blackmail continuing into the present. He put down his ballpoint and looked into Masao's eyes. "Can you prove the blackmail?"

"Yes." Masao picked up a parcel he'd placed under his chair. He unfolded the cotton wrap printed with a half-moon motif and placed a tape on the desk. "Here, Inspector-san. The last few times Togawa came to collect I taped his voice with a very nice little machine that cost me a lot of bread—I had to buy it on time. I put the recorder behind the screen and hid the microphone in a flower arrangement. Togawa never caught on. The quality of the recording is suberb. It contains a lot of bull, of course, because Togawa likes to talk and he always wants a drink too. We had regular ceremonies every month and afterward I would give him the money—but never freely, he always had to ask for it. Then he would thank me and count it. That's on the tape too, rustle rustle, a very clear microphone, you know, you can actually hear him touch the money. How's that for proof? Why don't you play it?"

Saito looked at his watch. It was almost lunchtime and he was more interested in getting that corpse out. "Later, Masao-san."

Masao got up and bowed. "You will be impressed by the tape, Inspector-san, and Togawa cannot deny that it's his voice. Are you going to arrest him?"

Saito bowed too. "You'll hear from us. I have your address, and I know where we can find Togawa-san."

"If he isn't home he usually hangs out in the Butterfly Bar, giving my money to the girls. That joint is much too expensive for the likes of us, but Togawa is a big shot these days. His business is going well and he's got half my wages on top of it. But that part's all over now. I paid him for the last time yesterday. Do you think I can get some of it back, Inspector-san?"

"You'll hear from us," Saito said again and walked his guest as far as the elevator. When the door closed after Masao he walked back to his office, shaking his head.

"Good evening, Masao," said the attractive girl who welcomed him to the Butterfly Bar. She led the way and he appraised her with pleasure. Nice girl, thought Masao. Maybe I'll get to know her better tonight, unless they have others that are even better-looking. He had paid a lot of attention to his appearance and was dressed in a dark suit, white shirt, and necktie. He had shaved carefully and brushed his nails as well as he could—there was only a little dirt left in the corners.

Sitting down on a barstool, he ordered a double Suntori whiskey. The girl, dressed in a hand-painted kimono with parallel orange stripes which accentuated her trim body, smiled and brought him a dish of nuts. Masao called to the bartender, "Give my girl friend something tasty."

He and the girl were getting on well when Togawa entered the bar and Masao regretted having to interrupt the conversation.

Togawa grinned widely: "Well, what do you know? This is quite a surprise, old buddy—let's see what you're drinking. Bartender, let me have one of those and another for my friend."

The girl got up and Togawa took over her stool. "Drop in on us again when you have time, darling," he said.

"Of course I will. Have a good time together—you must be old friends."

"You're dead right," Masao said. The strong liquor was already affecting him. His cheeks puffed out under his bulging eyes.

Togawa laughed. "You've been at it for a little while, I see. Are you celebrating something?"

Masao raised his drink. "I wasn't—but it's different now that you're here."

"That's the way I like to hear it," Togawa said. "We were friends, we stay friends. You know, I expected you to be here—isn't that strange? You never come here, but tonight I expected to see you. When I was walking here I thought, Masao is coming tonight too. I was quite sure of it."

"Is that a fact?" said Masao.

"Yes—so you see what good friends we are? I'm completely tuned in to you. Well, what shall we do? Have a party? Tonight everything is on me—just tell me what you want and I'll take care of it."

Masao laughed so hard he choked. The bar girl hit him on the back and Togawa got him a glass of water.

"Boy," whispered Masao, rubbing his eyes, "I haven't had so much fun in a long time. The way you said that. So you'll order me anything I want, right? Maybe I'll find you something too, a nice quiet little room where you can amuse yourself."

"Easy," Togawa said, "or you'll choke again. Come on, let's have another drink."

They drank a toast and became merrier, giggling at the slightest excuse.

The girls at the next bar got up to welcome them. "Kampai, first drink on the house to celebrate the coming spring. What will the gentlemen's pleasure be?"

Masao had recuperated from his first flush of drunkenness and stood steadily on his short legs, but Togawa had gone down into the nebulous spheres. When he tried to hold on to one of the girls while he ordered more whiskey, the girl disengaged herself and he almost fell over but managed to grab on to a tall slender man who had just entered the bar. "Sorry, sir—" he apologized. "The floor here seems to be slanting."

"Good evening," said Inspector Saito. Togawa turned and asked the girl where the rest room was. The inspector and Masao watched him make his way carefully to the room and struggle with the door's handle.

"What a coincidence," Saito said. "I went to your house but your landlady said you had gone out. When I got to the Butterfly Bar you had just left, and there are so many bars around here I didn't think I'd be able to find you."

Masao shook his broad head. "I'm glad to see you, Inspector." He pointed to the rest room door. "That's him, Inspector. Are you going to arrest him?"

"Maybe," said Saito, and took the glass the bartender pushed across the counter. "But we can take care of that matter later. Let's have a little chat with him first—or, even better, *you* talk to him and I'll listen. Tell him that he can't blackmail you anymore because your crime would be outdated. Look out, here he comes."

"Oh-oh," Togawa greeted Masao. "I better watch it, old buddy. I'm getting really drunk. I'll finish this one and maybe have one more, but then I think we should close the tap. How're you doing?"

"Not badly," Masao said. "Kampai. Let's drink to saying farewell."

Togawa stared at Masao glassily. "Farewell?"

"That's the word, buddy—or don't you know the law?" Masao pounded the counter with every word. *"All civilians are required to know the law."*

"Law? What law?"

"The law, old buddy of mine. Manslaughter cannot be prosecuted after twelve years. Twelve years ago I beat that bloody bastard to death. I did it without thinking about it, on the spur of the moment—that makes it manslaughter. Murder is valid for eighteen years, but it wasn't a murder. That swipe with the crowbar doesn't count anymore because twelve years have passed."

"Is that so?"

"Yes, it's so. But now *you're* in for it. Blackmail is a crime too, and you're still doing it. That's punishable, brother. It'll take you to jail for a long time. And all that time you can think of me. I'll be in a nice bar with lovely ladies while the rats are nibbling your toes."

"Never," Togawa said.

"Oh, yes."

Togawa moved his stool a little closer to Masao's. "Listen here, buddy, you know what's wrong with you? You're stupid. There's nothing in your fat stupid skull. In there." He tried to put his finger against Masao's forehead. "Sorry, that's your nose—but you don't have any brains there either. You don't have any savvy anywhere. So I blackmailed you for twelve years—you should never have let me get away with it. You killed—what's his name again? Takegaki?—because you were angry with him. How come you could never be that angry with me? Because you were too scared of me. To kill me you must be able to think and you can't. So you paid instead—every month, right on time. A stupid sucker, that's what you are."

Masao grinned. "Well, this stupid sucker is all done with you now and you can go to jail. Won't that be nice?"

"There's nothing you can do to me," Togawa said. "Blackmail's got to be proved, you know that much. Why don't you try to prove that you gave me half your wages every month just so I'd keep my mouth shut?"

"But I have beautiful proof. I have a whole tape filled with your voice and that tape is on a police inspector's desk right now."

Togawa roared with laughter. "Is that so? And do you know what that silly pig will be listening to? He'll be listening to Dreamy Doku, the pop singer, with electric organ in the background. You never bothered to play that tape back this morning, did you?"

Masao's mouth hung open.

"No, you took it to the police as fast as you could, just like I knew you would. Did you really think I wasn't aware you hid a tape recorder in your room? Do you know where I was last night while you were snoring away? I was right next to you, replacing your tape with mine. I know exactly what brand of tapes you use because I checked them when you left the room for a moment last time I was there. Togawa doesn't take any risks, buddy."

Inspector Saito looked at his watch. It was 11:30. He touched the bartender's hand. "Do me a favor, will you? Call the police. Tell them Inspector Saito is asking for assistance and that the matter is urgent."

The bartender nodded, pulled a telephone toward him, and dialed the number. Togawa and Masao were shouting at each other and the bar girls were trying to calm them down.

When two uniformed officers came in, the bartender pointed to Saito.

"Did you have us called, Inspector-san?"

"Yes." Saito got up and put a hand on Togawa's shoulder. "Togawa-san, I am Inspector Saito." He showed his badge. "I am arresting you on suspicion of blackmail. Would you please follow these two officers?"

"Handcuffs, Inspector?" asked one of the cops.

"Yes," Saito said, "why not?"

The officers pushed Togawa off his seat and the handcuffs clicked. "Where do you want him, Inspector-san?"

"Take him to Headquarters and tell the sergeant at the desk I'll be there in half an hour."

"Right, sir."

Togawa's legs seemed to be paralyzed as the policemen took him off and Masao turned to Saito. "Did I perform the way you expected me to, Saito-san? The bastard never knew what hit him."

"Yes, you did very well. Togawa is clever all right, but he shouldn't drink so much."

"So there's justice, after all," Masao said. "I was beginning to doubt it, you know. How I've longed for this moment—not to have to pay any more, and Togawa in jail!"

Saito looked at his watch again. "Yes, I can imagine your satisfaction, but I'm sorry, I'll have to arrest you too."

Masao didn't seem to hear. Saito raised his voice a little. "You're under arrest, Masao-san. I suspect you of killing your colleague, Takegaki. I arrived late tonight because it did indeed take us some time to get through to the corpse. But it was exactly where you indicated it would be. We found the crowbar you used buried with the corpse and have no reason to doubt that matters occurred the way you described them."

"But the whole thing is outdated!" shouted Masao. "That was twelve years ago! There's nothing you can do to me!"

Saito held his watch in front of Masao's eyes. "It's five to twelve, you see? In five minutes it will be March first and you can no longer be prosecuted. But you *can* be today, and we are prosecuting you because you committed your crime less than twelve years ago. We are still in the twelfth year. It is the twenty-ninth of February today, and there has been a small and very understandable oversight on your part. Leap year unsettles all of us and we forget about the extra day. My car is outside. You're going with me. I advise you not to resist, because that will only aggravate your position. Can I have the check, bartender? For the gentlemen and myself."

⧽⧽⧽ 8 ⧸⧸⧸

SAITO AND THE TWENTY-SEN STAMP

IF, SAITO THOUGHT, I REALLY AM AS EXTRAORDINARILY intelligent as the Police Academy teachers unanimously stated, then what am I doing in this impossible little room? There's snow on the ground and the park of the former Imperial Palace is close by. I could be walking between graceful pine trees and ancient, lovely buildings. No civilian will be committing a serious crime at this time of the morning. I'll wait for the water to boil, have tea, and be on my way.

He pulled the mini-hibachi carefully toward him, spooned green tea powder into a cracked cup, poured the steaming water, and made the tea foam by stirring it vigorously with an old chopstick.

"Yes?"

Kobori marched in, stopped and bowed. "Morning, Inspector-san."

Saito sighed and pushed the cup to the edge of his

desk. "Morning, Sergeant. I thought you had night duty. Please sit down and have some tea."

Kobori placed his cap, visor forward, under the chair's tatty straw seat and lowered himself carefully. He picked up the cup with both hands and watched the inspector over its edge. "Yes, Saito-san, I should be home by now but I thought I'd better report first."

Kobori's antique good manners improved Saito's mood. He opened a drawer of his desk, found a second cup, and once again busied himself with the tea ceremony. When he was done he looked at the sergeant again, noting that the sergeant, in spite of a long night's work, looked as crisp as his uniform that seemed to have just been torn out of the dry cleaner's plastic cover.

Kobori waited until Saito had taken his first sip. "Inspector-san; there was a fire in the Kitayama Quarter. An old man, a certain Mr. Nogi, suffocated. I have submitted my report and thought that the matter had been taken care of, but a certain aspect still bothers me."

Saito nodded. "Let's have it."

Kobori cleared his throat. "Right, Saito-san. It was like this. The fire wasn't exactly spectacular and the firemen took care of it in no time at all but Mr. Nogi died all the same. He was home by himself as his housekeeper, Setsuko, had gone out for a walk. Nogi was admiring his stamp collection in the upstairs room and was probably drunk—we found an empty sake bottle under his table. The wastepaper basket behind him caught fire and the flames ignited the floormats. It may be that Nogi-san nodded off after he emptied his ashtray into the basket. Rather a wasted little man, Saito-san; according to the housekeeper the master suffered from stomach trouble. A retired petty official of the city's administration, seventy years old and a lifelong bachelor."

"Who alerted the fire department?"

"A neighbor across the road, Mrs. Ichiyo, who wanted to admire moonlight on snow and saw flames licking at the upstairs window."

"And the housekeeper was out for a walk. What time did she come back?"

"At midnight. She had been out for an hour, to the gardens of the Daitokuji temple which is quite close. She said she couldn't sleep and it was indeed a beautiful night."

"Out by herself?"

"Yes, Saito-san."

"An attractive woman?"

Kobori nodded. "Thirty years old, a provincial lady, from Hokkaido. They talk kind of strangely out there. I had some trouble catching what she said."

"Do you think that Mr. Nogi was a wealthy man?"

"No, but not poor either. The house looked neat."

"Could his album be worth money?"

"Perhaps, it was completely filled with stamps."

Saito lit a cigarette and played with his telephone cord. "But it was still there, and the fire was caused by carelessness. But I take it you aren't sitting here to keep me company. What haven't you told me, Sergeant?"

Kobori's sharply featured head hinged a centimeter forward and his deepset eyes peered worriedly into Saito's. "That housekeeper was frightened and she didn't strike me as a nervous type. It couldn't have been my fault for I hadn't been harassing her and the constable I happened to have with me is a most peaceful man. The doctor immediately confirmed that Nogi had indeed been suffocated by smoke and he had left with the corpse before

Setsuko returned. I merely asked her the normal questions, whether the dead man had any relatives and if she intended to leave the house unattended but she trembled and stuttered and it seemed that she could become aggressive any moment, like an animal that feels itself trapped. While I interrogated her I thought that she might perhaps be in shock because her life had so suddenly changed... no more work... perhaps she was fond of the old man ...but later, after leaving my report at the desk I began to wonder about the whole thing."

"Do you know if there is an heir?"

"A nephew who lives in Osaka." Kobori pulled a notebook from his side pocket and noted an address in tight square characters. He tore the page free and put it on Saito's desk. "Perhaps you could visit Setsuko-san today, if you have a minute, Inspector-san. She told me that she worked for the deceased for over a year, and before that in some restaurant."

Chief Inspector Ikemiya waited at the open elevator door but Saito didn't move. Ikemiya gestured invitingly. "Aren't you getting out?"

"Forgot something," Saito mumbled and moved over to make space for his superior's ample body. The chief inspector nudged his assistant. "At it that early already? They told me at the desk that nothing happened last night."

"A fire," Saito said tonelessly.

The elevator stopped. "Fire," said Ikemiya in the corridor, "since when do we waste our time with fires?"

"A fire and a corpse."

"Burned corpse?"

"Choked corpse."

Ikemiya looked aside irritably. "Yes? Can happen, can't

it? Smoke kills too." He stopped and grabbed hold of Saito's arm. "Say, you wouldn't have information that passed me by, would you?"

"Don't know yet." Saito pulled himself free. "Excuse me, this is my office. You'll hear from me, Ikemiya-san, if there is anything further to report."

Saito waited until Ikemiya's door banged at the end of the corridor before he picked up a book that had been wrapped in a piece of gold-embroidered silk and took it out of its cover. Case 16B, now how did that go? He found the chapter and read aloud: "'When Yen Tsun was prefect of Yang-chou he once made an inspection journey through the district that had been entrusted to him. He suddenly heard someone shout out in fear rather than sadness. He had his chariot stopped and interrogated the person. She answered: "My husband had an accident with fire and died." Yen Tsun suspected her and ordered a constable to investigate the corpse. He saw that flies gathered around the head's crown and looked: he found the head of an iron nail that had been hammered into the skull. It was proved that the woman, together with her paramour, had killed her husband and the suspects confessed.'"

Ikemiya entered without knocking and stood next to Saito. His fleshy hand hit the desk edge. "No, Saito, not again. How often do I have to tell you that what happened in antique China has nothing to do with modern Japan?" He stared accusingly at his subordinate. "Times have changed, Inspector. We use computers today and know what happens on planets that the naked eye can hardly see. How can we learn anything from moldy magistrates who had nothing to apply but their intuition and who utilized a whip to obtain confessions?"

Saito observed his chief quietly. Ikemiya produced a handkerchief and blew his nose. "Damned snow has given me a cold. Now tell me what's wrong with your corpse. Do we have a case? And if so, do you plan working on it?"

Saito folded the book back into its silken wrap. "Sergeant Kobori thinks that the dead man's housekeeper behaved in an unusual manner and I was thinking I might go and see her."

"Tell me what you know."

Saito reported.

Ikemiya extended a hand. "I stopped smoking but this nonsense is too much. Give me a cigarette, Inspector." He inhaled deeply and blew out the smoke, coughing sharply. "Bah, a rich aristocrat like yourself who considers his work a hobby should allow himself a better brand. And what sort of a motive for a possible murder would you suggest?"

"I don't know yet."

Ikemiya regarded his glowing cigarette. "Nothing seems to be missing, you said. An emotional conflict? Nogi was a sickly old chap and Setsuko is an attractive young woman. It has been ascertained that old lechers tend to abuse their servants but a wench from Hokkaido isn't my idea of a pushover." He shrugged. "Perhaps you should have a look at her. Spending an hour with a handsome maiden might be more fun than reading dusty files here." He rubbed his stub in the ashtray. "But don't get carried away by youthful enthusiasm. We're here to keep things quiet and not to add to the confusion."

Saito let the staff car and driver go and compared the address with Kobori's note. Except for a few sparrows arguing in the gutter nothing moved in the tiny street. The house seemed hardly damaged, only the paper in the upstairs window had been torn. He pushed the gate open and walked to the door, which slid aside as soon as he called good morning.

"Setsuko-san?"

Her gaze was steady. "At your service."

He thought that her simple kimono and starched apron did indeed give her a rather provincial appearance. "I'm a police officer, Miss, and here to make a routine check. That's customary when there has been a deadly accident. Can I come in, please?"

She guided him to the front room, arranged a cushion to sit on, and knelt opposite him on the worn mat. Her hands pulled at the hem of her apron. Saito smiled encouragingly. "I hear that you have been working for Mr. Nogi for more than a year. Is that right, Setsuko-san?"

"Yes, eh, yes."

"And you were a waitress in a restaurant before. Did Mr. Nogi meet you there?"

Her facial muscles hardened and she had trouble formulating her answer. "That's what I said." Her hand brushed impatiently across her face.

"How do you mean, 'That's what I said'? Wasn't it true?"

Tears dribbled slowly toward her high cheekbones, her shoulders shook, and her hands plucked frantically at her clothing. "No."

"You didn't work in a restaurant?"

She swallowed and shot him a desperate look. "I shouldn't have said that. I knew you would find out the truth."

"What truth?"

"That I used to be a photo model."

"Photo model," Saito said pensively. "Right. And Mr. Nogi? How did you get to know your employer?"

"In the studio of course, behind the Raku Hotel."

Saito recalled the low-class hotel. What could be found in the neighborhood behind the Raku? Exactly, porno studios, rickety little wooden buildings where women allowed themselves to be photographed in any way the client specified, for a small fee. "And you were ashamed to divulge that information to the policemen who came here last night?"

"Yes."

"I see. Mr. Nogi visited you often in the studio and offered you a job in the end. Is that correct?

"Yes."

"So you weren't just a housekeeper?"

She pointed at the low ceiling. "We slept together, upstairs."

"Did you mind putting up with the old man?"

She brushed a strand of hair that had escaped from the ornamental comb keeping her topknot together. "Not really, he didn't expect much."

"You were paid well?"

"Some, but I never managed to save. He only ate boiled rice and wouldn't let me cook for myself because the smell made him hungry. To eat outside all the time costs a lot of money."

Saito produced his cigarette pack. "Care for a smoke, Setsuko-san?"

"No, smoking is unhealthy. Mr. Nogi smoked too and the doctor said he shouldn't."

"Do you mind if I smoke?"

She got up and took a dish from a shelf. She stumbled

and almost fell when she knelt again. "Here, for your ashes."

"And he drank, didn't he?"

"No."

"No?"

She clapped her hand over her mouth. "Yes, he did, sometimes."

Saito sucked his cigarette thoughtfully. "Tell me, how did Nogi-san spend his time?"

Her apron strap had become undone and her hands trembled when she redid the knot. "He walked about the quarter and during the evenings he usually played with his stamps or we watched TV."

Saito got up. "May I see the upstairs room, please?"

She led the way on the narrow staircase and he admired the seductive shape of her firm body, accentuated by the tight kimono. *It was proved that the woman, together with her paramour, had killed her husband and the suspects confessed.*

She bowed awkwardly. "This is the room where Nogi-san died."

"Another question. You did lie to us before so please don't hold it against me if I am a little suspicious. Tell me, were you and Mr. Nogi married, perhaps?"

She grinned nervously. "No, he didn't want to. I said we should get married so that he wouldn't have to waste money on wages anymore but he didn't want me to inherit the house. His nephew in Osaka has sons who are supposed to go to university later on. He said I should be able to take care of myself."

"That wasn't very nice of him, was it?"

"No."

"And what are your plans now, Setsuko-san?"

She bit her finger before answering. "I don't know yet."

"You have no relatives?"

"No, nobody."

"No brothers, no sisters?"

"No one." She suddenly looked angry and he dropped his gaze. The room showed clear signs of the fire. A floormat had changed into a mass of ashes and the table and the rolled-up bedding in a corner were covered with a yellowish flaky substance, remnants of the fire brigade's foam. He touched a sake bottle with the tip of his shoe. "Mr. Nogi shouldn't have imbibed strong rice wine. Sake is pure poison for people who have stomach trouble."

She didn't comment. He looked up and saw how she had pressed herself against the wall. Her breathing was laborious and her clawed hands scratched on the material of her apron. He became aware of a sharp stench of fresh sweat.

He turned away and bowed toward the table. "Aha, here is the stamp album. Maybe I should take it with me." He shook a visiting card from his wallet, put it on the table, and picked up the album. "If Mr. Nogi's nephew should come you can tell him he can retrieve this at Headquarters."

The woman still seemed stuck to the wall. Saito nodded pleasantly. "I better be on my way. Goodbye, Setsuko-san."

Chief Inspector Ikemiya frowned furiously. He had adjusted his revolving chair to its sharpest angle and kicked off his shoes. His feet rested on a stack of law books. Saito studied the energetic toes of his chief, moving about gaily within the thin cotton of the fairly worn socks.

"You don't exactly obey your instructions," grumbled Ikemiya. "I thought I had asked you not to bother that woman unnecessarily. Why did she have to be arrested? The constables told me that she didn't come easily and one of them had to go to the emergency room to have his face treated. Couldn't you have taken her yourself if you wanted the suspect locked up?"

"That wouldn't have been a good move."

"No?" Ikemiya's heavy eyebrows wriggled sarcastically. "You weren't frightened of that dreadful harpie, were you? I thought you were such a hero on the judo mat."

Saito smiled politely. "I wasn't in uniform and I had made the mistake of sending the car away. If a man drags a handsome woman along the street passersby tend to interfere."

Ikemiya's big toe peeped through the sock's fresh hole. Saito grinned. Ikemiya yanked his feet back.

"Saito," whispered Ikemiya hoarsely, "this time you have really gone too far. That woman is innocent. Haven't you seen the coroner's report? Alcohol in the blood and smoke in the lungs. That old codger was as drunk as a coot, whether you think that the woman lied or not, and he did choke on smoke. That balderdash you are trying to make me swallow, that Case 16B taken out of context from a primeval manual on catching idiots, is drivel. The 16B corpse had a nail in his noggin but your corpse had breathed smoke. That scientifically proven fact tells us that he wasn't killed before the fire occurred." Ikemiya's hairy fist hit the desk top. "*No* indication that violence was applied. Confirmation that the housekeeper spoke the truth. So what do we do? We throw the lady in a cell." He held up a piece of paper. "You know what this is?"

"A letter?" Saito asked softly.

"Right, signed by Chief of Police Gato. The boss wants to know whether I truly think that we have suffcient serious suspicions to warrant the suspect Setsuko's arrest. So what do you suggest I should answer, eh?"

"That we do have sufficient serious suspicions," Saito said evenly. "I visited the neighbor Ichiyo, the lady across the street from the Nogi residence. The witness states that she knew Nogi well and often talked to him. She swears that Nogi hasn't enjoyed a drop of alcohol since he was operated on a year ago for bleeding of the stomach."

"Bah, that's what he told her. Alcoholics are professional liars."

"And Mrs. Ichiyo also told me about the brother of housekeeper Setsuko."

Ikemiya groaned and stuck out his hand. Saito filled it with a cigarette. Ikemiya pressed his silver desk lighter. He inhaled deeply. "Brother?"

"Yes, Chief Inspector-san. Setsuko said she was quite alone in the world but her brother visited her regularly. Mr. Nogi was quite fond of the young man and described him as both intelligent and eager to learn."

"That Ichiyo madam claims all that? And you believe..."

"That the so-called brother was Setsuko's lover."

"And that, quite according to Case 16B, the loving couple did away with poor helpless Mr. Nogi." Ikemiya's fist banged on the armrest of his chair. "And why, if I may ask, Mr. Genius? To steal the gold bars carefully hidden by Nogi? Since when do retired minor officials dispose of secret wealth? Nothing was missing, was it? Even that silly stamp album had not been disturbed. You really want us to be shown up as nitwits? If the law is applied literally we can be accused of illegally harassing a citizen."

Saito shook his head. "I don't think so, Ikemiya-san. The suspect has weakened her position considerably by telling lies."

"So whàt do you want now?"

Saito jumped up. "Pry a little further. I think we should be able to come up with something tangible today."

The thin scarecrow behind the stamp store's counter, surrounded by carelessly stacked boxes and stockbooks, tore himself free from his daydreams and bowed to Saito. Saito greeted him, placed the album on the littered counter, and presented his card.

The storekeeper's mouth dropped open. "You are an inspector of the Criminal Investigation Department?"

Saito nodded. "We would value your advice. This collection interests us; it's an item involved in a serious case. Perhaps you could spare a few minutes to study its contents."

The dealer's thin lips curved into a sardonic grin. "You wouldn't be after a free appraisal, would you now, Mr. Official?"

"Not at all," Saito said quietly. "Quite honestly I don't know what I am after, but you're an expert. All I can see is that the collection is complete. I trust that your remarks will give me better clues."

"Complete," the storekeeper mumbled, and switched on a strong light while he opened the album. "Don't see that very often. Either the owner is old or he is rich. The old stamps aren't available anymore but that modern stuff comes out of the machines by the millions and can be bought anywhere at any price you like. Here, the nineteenth century, that's what matters, you know."

Saito followed the spindly finger that caressed the page.

"Here they are," the dealer whispered almost reverently. "The 1874 series, with the imperial chrysanthemum as the chief decoration. The stamps of four, six, twenty, and thirty sen. The sen was worth something then and a hundred fitted into a yen; now even a yen won't buy you a sliver of dried fish. Can I take them out, Inspector-san?"

"Please."

The storekeeper opened a drawer and produced a pair of tweezers and a magnifier equipped with a focused light. He switched the gadget on and pulled the twenty-sen stamp, an unsightly lilac-colored bit of irregularly notched paper, carefully from the album. "They come on thick paper, and then we are likely to pay a bit, and they come on thin paper, in which case we empty out the purse. On thin paper this darling is worth three and a half million, dear sir, and the collectors will pay that much too, for the series is harder to get all the time. Ah, just look at this."

"A little tear?" Saito was peering at what the dealer dangled in front of his eyes.

"You can see that without spectacles? You are a happy man."

The storekeeper rummaged in his drawer again and came up with cut lenses attached to a small clasp. He clipped them on his glasses. "Right, now let's take another peek."

The sudden flow of abuse was pronounced with such venom that Saito staggered away from the counter.

"Rubbish, utter rubbish," the dealer yelled. "Torn and glued. Worthless junk. That's the way the fool who's after completeness crooks himself. What does he care as long as his album is full? The twenty sen on thin paper, the rarity we all look for and it finally pops up; you're ready to thank the Goddess of Mercy and it's damaged so you've still got nothing."

"Why don't you look further?" Saito asked. "So this one is bad but there may be others."

"A pile of waste," the storekeeper said sadly. "Fool's gold. Hey, what do we have here?" He pressed his magnifier on the other three stamps of the series and pulled on the goatee that pretended to hide his lack of chin. "Well now, these seem to lie in excellent order, on thick paper of course, but even so they should be worth a couple of thousand." He moved his instrument and scrutinized the rest of the page. "Here, very nice too, three thousand maybe, and here again, prime quality, I would say." He turned the page and continued to nod approvingly. "First class, not a bad collection after all." He took off his glasses and smiled at Saito. "Cup of tea, Inspector-san? This work always makes me thirsty. I go through half a gallon a day and my throat stays dry."

"You don't want to study the others?"

"You want me to? The new stuff is boring, I think. It's only the old ones that cheer me up. I'll put those four back again before they get lost."

The dealer rehooked his spectacles over his ears and flipped back to the page where he had started. "Strange, don't you think? Why would that one stamp, the only one that really matters, be in such a miserable condition? If it had been all right it would have been worth a hundred times more than all the rest of the collection together. Hmm. I say!"

"You see something?"

"Man wants to know if I see something." The store-keeper's complicated glasses nearly touched the page. "I certainly do. There must have been a protector here, and it was ripped out with force. The marks are clear enough." The tip of his index finger rubbed the damaged paper. "You know what that is, a protector?"

"No."

"I'll explain it to you. See here, they come in strips of double clear plastic so that the stamps can be inserted between the two layers. Once the stamp is in you cut the strip with a pair of scissors so that you get a nice protector that fits the stamp exactly. There's strong glue on the back; you lick it and you press stamp and protector into the album." He pushed his body away from the counter and stretched leisurely. "But those strips are fairly pricey and the customer usually prefers cheap hinges that he can buy for next to nothing per thousand. Protectors are only used for special stamps, or for new ones when the gummed sides should remain undamaged."

Saito closed the album, stuck it under his arm, and bowed.

"No tea?" the dealer asked. "My tea is famous in the street. A cup will do you good, especially when you have to face the cold again."

Saito had reached the door. "Thank you, some other time perhaps. I appreciate your help."

Saito stopped outside to enjoy the fresh air before walking on, along show windows that held stamps and their appurtenances. A sign dangling from iron hooks reminded him that it was lunchtime. The small restaurant's interior was crowded but he managed to find an empty stool and ordered a dish of fried rice garnished with pickled radish.

He observed the guests while he ate. Most of them were elderly gentlemen drinking tea and nibbling seaweed cookies while they discussed the contents of one another's stockbooks. Stamps held by tweezers flitted across table-tops; the café seemed to house an eternal exchange. A poster attached to the counter propagated a stamp magazine and informed the public that single copies were available. Saito asked the waitress to bring him the magazine and glanced through the pages while he slurped his tea. Except for some articles, illustrated with color photographs of stamps, the magazine contained a number of advertisements offering the services of mail order companies and specialized stores. He saw that the Kyoto-based dealers preferred a certain street, the street he happened to be in now. He sighed while he redlined the ads. A total of eight; he hoped he had enough time. He paid, clasped the album under his arm, and left the restaurant.

Fortune only smiled at the fifth store. The owner, a small fat fellow with a kindly face, bowed helpfully. "Yes, Inspector, I do remember a repaired lilac twenty-sen stamp of 1874. I found it in a box with leftovers that I picked up cheaply at an auction and jumped for joy."

Saito grinned. "Before you saw that the stamp was worthless."

The owner whacked himself on the forehead. "Indeed. What a disappointment! The chance you have been praying for and Heaven frowns on you after all."

"What did you do with the stamp?"

"I kept it as a curiosity for a while but I gave it away in the end to a student who had been helping out here for a few weeks. He was a bit of a collector himself and he craved the stamp because it would give some color to an otherwise empty page."

"Do you remember his name?"

The owner's skull had to be thick, for the resounding slap he cheerfully gave himself hardly made him blink. "You're a policeman, I clean forgot. That nice young man wouldn't be in trouble, I hope?"

Saito's smile faded away. "He could very well be. Is he a friend of yours?"

"Friend, friend, but he was a hard worker and I liked him. Wakana, the name is, a clever young lad, has to be since he told me he was a candidate of mathematics. Haven't got his address, I'm afraid."

"Can you describe him?"

The owner thought for a moment. "Yes, a small nimble sort of chap but wide-shouldered and with a strange way of walking. Always reminded me of those puppets they sell at fairs, the type with a key in their backs, but with Wakana you didn't have to turn the key—he jumped by himself."

Saito had to restrain himself not to rush out of the store. The description fitted with what Mrs. Ichiyo had told him about Setsuko's brother.

Ikemiya pointed disdainfully at the stamp that Saito had placed on his desk. "That miserable little rag? Three and a half million yen?"

"Yes, sir, the price of a comfortable house or a sum that, properly invested, will keep a modest man going just on the interest. You will admit that a valuable object like this could constitute a motive for murder."

Ikemiya indicated the chair that he reserved for important visitors. "Sit down, Inspector, and tell me exactly how you concluded your case. I take it that the report and signed confessions will reach me in due course but we might go through the case verbally now. Fire away, Saito-san."

Saito relaxed in his leather-upholstered seat. "Yes, but first of all I should state that I would never have considered the case if Kobori hadn't insisted that I should. My visit to Mr. Nogi's house only confirmed the sergeant's original suspicion. Setsuko's blatant lie about Nogi-san's drinking habits was the next indication and I began to suspect that the murderers—"

Ikemiya's protesting hand jumped from the desk's blotter. "One moment, Saito. I don't follow how you could, at that early stage of the game, surmise that Setsuko hadn't perpetrated the foul deed by herself."

Saito smiled. "*Parallel Cases Under the Pear Tree*, the thirteenth-century manual that I habitually use when I busy myself with detection. I'll fetch the book if you like and read you the relevant passage."

Ikemiya waved the suggestion away. "Save yourself the effort, I know that passage by heart, I'm sure."

"Even in the old days," Saito said solemnly, "magistrates knew that stupid unevolved women, and Setsuko is a classic example of the type, do not easily commit serious crimes by themselves. If they do misbehave a male master has set them off and uses the female as an accomplice. When I interrogated Setsuko I noticed at once that she had little intelligence and I decided that she would have played a lesser part in the drama. She would have met a great many men when she worked as a porno model and it is unlogical to assume that they would all have been elderly gentlemen like Mr. Nogi. She must have found a lover and the affair continued after she moved in with Nogi."

"Suppositions," Ikemiya said bad-temperedly, "without any factual evidence."

Saito nodded patiently. "Certainly, but my idea was a useful hypothesis for the time being. All I had to do was look for facts and try to fit them in with my theory. If they wouldn't fit, the hypothesis would have to be replaced by another and—"

"Yes, save me the lecture. What happened then?"

"I heard that a young man had been visiting the Nogi residence and that the master of the house had called him both intelligent and eager to learn. I asked myself what Nogi, a retired clerk, could have taught his promising disciple. The old man's only hobby was stamp collecting. It seemed clear that he had showed off his album and that Wakana had shown considerable interest."

Ikemiya's fingers drummed on the blotter. "Right, very possible. Carry on."

"Lover and beloved killed old Mr. Nogi. Why? To benefit from the situation. What did Mr. Nogi own? A house and furniture, objects that are hard or even impossible to steal. He also owned a stamp album which had not been taken. I took the collection to an expert who noticed that the only really valuable stamp, the 1874 twenty-sen lilac chrysanthemum, was damaged and therefore worthless while all other stamps were in excellent condition."

"So you had to find the original. You did, for it is here on my desk. How..."

Saito held up his cigarettes. "You're still not smoking?"

Ikemiya sucked the smoke hungrily, "Well?"

"That particular stamp is very rare and even damaged copies are hard to find. Every dealer who ever handled a copy would be sure to remember the occasion. I called on the local stamp stores and one dealer told me that he had once given a torn twenty-sen stamp to a student of mathematics who had worked in his store. Then I knew enough. Nogi's stamp had only been removed last night and the thief would still be in possession of the missing object, for he was surely clever enough not to try to sell the stamp locally, since he was known to the dealers. I telephoned the university's administration and obtained his address. I then collected Sergeant Kobori and went to Wakana's room."

"Was he home?"

"No, but we didn't have to wait too long. When he showed up he refused to let us in at first, saying that we should have a warrant, but we were still in the street and I threatened to arrest him on the spot."

"So you knew the stamp would be in his room."

"Clearly, why refuse to let us in otherwise? The trouble was exactly *where* in his room? Stamps are easily hidden. Fortunately Kobori is an experienced policeman and he observed the suspect while I asked some innocent questions. Kobori noticed that Wakana's eyes kept straying toward a photograph taken of Setsuko. The photograph must have dated from the time that she still worked in the studio because her pose was rather revealing. There were other pictures in the room and Wakana must have seen his girl friend's portrait a thousand times but its presence seemed to comfort him somehow."

"The stamp had been stuck to the photo's back?"

"We found it in the frame, between the actual photo and a piece of cardboard backing."

Ikemiya grinned contentedly. "Did Wakana confess straight off?"

"He refused to say anything for a while but broke down when, here in this building, I made him look through a cell-door's peephole. His spirit broke when he saw Set-suko."

"Did you tell him that his love had confessed already?"

Saito's voice shot up. "I certainly did not. Such meth-ods are beneath my sense of dignity."

Ikemiya sneered, "But you didn't say that she had *not* confessed, right?"

"I didn't tell him anything at all. I only wanted the suspect to realize that we had arrested his accomplice as well."

"Not to tell the truth is to lie too, Saito, but never mind that subtle point for now. We all know that suspects can easily be manipulated when kept in uncertainty. Now tell me how the actual murder was committed."

"Wakana and Setsuko grabbed hold of Mr. Nogi, pushed him on his back and forced him to drink half a bottle of strong sake."

"So he had really stopped drinking?"

"Yes, and after a year of abstention and with an ulcer-ous stomach such a dose can be deadly. Wakana knew that the coroner would look for smoke in the lungs and had devised a clever way of making sure that there was. He likes fishing and owns a pump to fill his small rubber dinghy with air. He lit a fire in Nogi's metal wastepaper basket, covered it with a wire rack, and placed the pump on the wire. That way the pump could be handled without him having to breathe in smoke himself. Setsuko stuck the tube as deeply as possible into Nogi's throat..."

Ikemiya scratched his underchin. "An interesting detail that will impress the judge. I don't think the suspects can claim extenuating circumstances. I hope you collected the pump; it would be nice to produce it as evidence."

"I did, and we have the wire rack too. Wakana couldn't

remember exactly where it could be found; he had dumped it in the little park at the end of Nogi's street. Kobori took a few men and managed to find it within half an hour."

"Very nice indeed. But something else bothers me, Saito. Why didn't that clever fellow steal the album outright? It was his intention that the house would burn to the ground and he couldn't know that your Ichiyo witness had picked that evening to admire moonlight on snow."

Saito nodded. "That point bothered me too. Wakana is a vain young man, however, and he took pleasure in supplying us with an answer. His landlady asked him to burn some debris in the yard of her house. The debris contained an old telephone book. It turned out that a fat book does not disappear in a fire but changes into a lump of brittle ashes that still show the original shape of the volume. Wakana was worried that the young Mr. Nogi, the heir, would try to find the remnants of the album to claim the value with the insurance company. Wakana also stated that as a promising student of mathematics he took pride in considering all possibilities. It was possible that the fire would be put out before the house burned down in which case the missing album might start off a police investigation."

Ikemiya sighed. "Quite, quite, and how did the suspect intend to change his loot into money?"

"He was going to wait until the next large stamp auction in Tokyo. Those auctions attract not only dealers but also wealthy collectors. He would have been sure to obtain the full price."

Ikemiya got up slowly. "I do believe that I have to congratulate you after all, Saito, even if you were incredibly lucky and your hypothesis had little to support it but thin air." He pushed the stamp away. "Don't forget to take this with you, before I sneeze and it's lost forever."

Saito bowed but the chief inspector gazed out of the window, seemingly having forgotten his inspector's existence.

‖‖ 9 ‖‖

MESSING ABOUT IN BOATS

ADRIAN DE ROOS, ADIRANO DOROSU AS PRONOUNCED in Japanese, Dutch professor of philosophy temporarily teaching in Japan, was not in a good mood. He walked ahead of Yoshiko, as dictated by local custom, and had her carry the lunchbasket. He also walked too fast and the girl, off balance on her high heels and hindered by her tight skirt, had trouble keeping up with the tall blonde-haired blue-eyed foreigner. "Dorosu-san, please, not so quickly," she called from time to time, in the wailing high little voice used by Japanese women when they surrender to a man. He would slow down a little, look over his shoulder, excuse himself, and forget again that he wasn't the only one on earth. He had wanted to spend the day reading, stretched out on two chairs, with a lot of cigarettes and an endless supply of coffee, but Yoshiko had been whining at him for months now so he might as well have the outing, and be done once and for all. He was about to spend time boating, together with the secretary

160

the university had been good enough to supply him with as part of his income, because in money he didn't earn all that much. That's the way it goes in Japan; a young professor can flatter himself on working for a renowned institute, he is given a free apartment, eats for a dime and a nickel in the canteen, everyone, the older professors excluded, bows deeply when he comes by, and he gets a bit of cash as well.

Good day to you, Adrian thought, he would rather take a lot of money. He wished he was still in Hong Kong; Chinese are practical folk, prepared to pay straight interest in western philosophy. Over there he had at least felt that he might be employed usefully and that his audience understood what he was talking about. Besides, he spoke good Chinese and now had trouble with Japanese. "Make sure you link up with an intelligent whore," the Chinese colleagues told him when he departed. "A foreign tongue is learned quickest on the pillow." He was also told there would be many prostitutes in Japan, as many at least as in Hong Kong.

Leaving wasn't too bad, arriving was. He had met enough bar girls by now; they all wanted a steady friend but he couldn't face the commitment. In Hong Kong it had been all right to flutter from flower to flower but here the pattern turned out to be more intricate. Even with Yoshiko, whom he hadn't touched with a finger yet, he felt caught by a thousand minute hooks, dug firmly into his flesh, working themselves in a little more every day. What was his relationship with the girl anyway? She typed his lectures, in correct English, and helped with the Japanese explanations, since he tried, every now and then, to teach in the local lingo. She had lunch with him and liked to "discuss philosophy." He would respond by always

taking the negative view so that he could succeed in strip-
ping whatever she came up with of any possible value—
a game he had learned at Leyden University while bar-
hopping with his fellow students. That he didn't always
believe in his own arguments was his business. He disliked the girl and enjoyed drilling holes in her limited
concepts.

Still, Yoshiko wasn't really bad looking, her body was
well shaped and her legs fairly straight, not bent as with
most Japanese females. That she wore spectacles shouldn't
bother him either; they could come off at the right
moments, couldn't they? And didn't she always make an
effort to be charming? She helped with his shopping, took
him to good restaurants, removed stains from his clothes.
If he didn't take care she would do anything. *Here I am,
Lord, abuse me. Shall I fetch the whip?* It so happened,
however, that he wasn't sadistically inclined. Or was he,
perhaps? It's risky to state about the self that it is *not*
something in particular. He had studied Jung, after all,
even with much zeal. Every man has a shadow that
accompanies him at all times and the shadow is the opposite of what a man thinks he is, hopes to be, insists on
believing himself to be. Adrian had always taken himself
to be a kindly disposed gentleman, so he could very well
be an utter scoundrel; just wait, the shadow slithers along
and is forever ready to prove its worth. Never mind,
Adrian thought, we're going boating now. He waited until
Yoshiko, panting, could catch up. "Dorosu-san, your legs
are so long and I'm only little, huh, huh, huh."

"*Sumimasen*, Yoshiko-san," Adrian said dutifully.
Wasn't he sorry that the poor little thing had run out of
breath? "But there are the nice boats waiting for us, dear,
see? Your ordeal is almost over."

The boat man shook his head when he saw Yoshiko's thin spiked heels. "My boats are made out of thin plastic, Miss, and they'll fill up in no time if you pierce the hull. There's quite a bit of wind today. There's another rental outfit further along—they have stronger boats."

"No," the girl said, clipping her words nastily, "I'll take off my shoes."

She had gotten in already and Adrian was rowing; the sharp nose of the sleek little craft cut through the waves.

"Ooooh," Yoshiko said. "You're so good at it. You can do everything well, can't you?"

"Can't you row?"

"No, I've hardly ever been on the water. We only used to go once in a while when I was a kid. On a pond that was, and my parents would come too. The water was shallow out there, but this is a real big lake. Shall we go to that island? We could have lunch on the beach."

Adrian looked over his shoulder; the island was some miles away. He saw a hill, suitably surrounded by what would be pine trees.

He rowed on with a vengeance. Three years in the country now and he still didn't like it. The paper-thin politeness that covered all behavior had a tendency to interfere with his breathing and he drank more than he had done even during his student years. Only in drunkenness will the Japanese open up, or so he was beginning to believe. How many more evenings would he still have to spend in artfully furnished bars, between the red grinning faces of his colleagues, assuring him of their everlasting friendship while they fondled the serving girls.

That miserable Yoshiko, would he ever be rid of her fawning approach? She was waiting for him at every corner; she had already stated her love, hiccuping with emotion, after much sake in a romantic inn. Pressed to the edge of a mental precipice, Adrian admitted that he preferred gentlemen to ladies. It wasn't quite true—his preference for the male sex was incidental—but he had to come up with something and it had better be final. Caught between the paper lanterns, with a view of a full moon detaching itself gently from the embrace of pine branches, could he have been expected to answer, "Yoshiko, you're abhorrent to me, the very sight of you turns me off completely"? He couldn't have said that, could he now?

"Does happiness exist, Dorosu-san?" Yoshiko asked him afterward. The idea! Since when has life been designed to point at happiness? Had he chosen the discipline of philosophy to become happy? He needed happiness as much as he needed love play with this poorly programmed plastic doll.

"I think so, Yoshiko."

"Have you been able to find it?"

"No." He said it sadly, swallowing the contents of another cup of rice wine, feeling the alcohol dull his perceptions—there wasn't much difference anymore between the lanterns painted with characters and the moon cut through by branches.

"So what is the purpose of human existence?"

"No purpose. Life is no more than senseless suffering."

She raised her hands in weak protest but he wasn't done yet. "Suicide, Yoshiko," Professor de Roos said solemnly, "is the only valid way out. And besides," he dropped his voice to a confidential whisper, "that way we can at least create an illusion of free will, and succeed in symbolizing our dignity."

"But you're alive."

"Out of weakness, Yoshiko, but I assure you that I

want nothing more than death." He paused significantly. "One day I may gather enough courage. A little more sake, Yoshiko? Drink up, alcohol is death too, and intoxication a splendid beginning."

Her foot touched his ankle under the table but he withdrew his leg.

The scene was crystal clear in his memory, while he pulled on the oars and the waves breaking across the bow drenched his back, but that evening had slid away long ago, and was no more than a part of an overall pool of misery.

She talked to him, like a mother talks to her infant, about the birds flying and swimming around them, the shoreline, partly shrouded in fog, the brilliant red color of a buoy floating by. He knew that she wasn't merely babbling nonsense, and that she might genuinely be impressed by the beauty of the environment, but why go into all those idiotic details?

Adrian's father had been "lost" in a World War II prison camp on the then Dutch island of Java. Starved to death, beaten senseless, who would ever know what the sadistic Japanese guards had done to Papa de Roos? And who would ever know how he, the holy father figure, would have behaved if the roles had been reversed? De Roos Senior as a camp guard, it could well have been possible. Adrian didn't remember his father as having been a pleasant man. One has to be careful with generalizations, transference, and idealism. Didn't Jung say, and probably rightly, that man has great potential for the highest good, and the worst evil? To be motivated now by open or hidden hatred would be a dangerous slip into nonconscious behavior. If only Yoshiko would shut up. The girl jabbered on, however. She looked inviting, he would say that much for her. The tight skirt had crept up to well above her knees, and her breasts, almost completely exposed in the low-cut blouse, were also hard to ignore. He promised himself to keep his hands off her. Two more years waited at the Kyoto University and a wrong move now would jeopardize future adventures in the Willow Quarter. All he had to do today was row, eat, listen to the girl's verbal flow of trivialities, and then home, Home.

"Careful, Dorosu-san, we're almost there."

He pulled the dory onto the rocky beach and Yoshiko unpacked the hamper, moving continuously, providing a selection of cleavage and seductive thighs for his perusal. She offered the food gracefully, illustrating each dish with embellished labels. Mushrooms from the famous island such and such, known for its autumn colors; seaweed cookies from the far northwest where the snow monkeys live; a salad of this and a fish stew of that; only the rice had to be plain, for rice is rice.

The rice wine was of exceptional origin again, and came with its own story and in a large stone jug, decorated with bright blue paper cord. It was a little early for cocktails but she insisted and poured cups for two, forcing more on him while she drank steadily herself. He was debating whether he would go back on his decision and grab her after all—why not anyway, surely he would find a way to be rid of her afterward—when he noticed that he wasn't only drunk but nauseous. His intestines cramped until he was in pain and he crawled away, aiming for a rock that seemed to offer protection. Yoshiko was also in trouble, and staggering about in the direction of another large boulder. Too much sake, Adrian thought, while he vomited and squatted down afterward. He should be used to the stuff now. He rolled away from his own stench and spent a few minutes on his back, breathing deeply, before forcing himself to walk back. The lunchbasket stood on an empty beach, its half-eaten contents waiting in pretty dishes on a reed mat. He found Yoshiko. She was crying.

"Feeling better? That sake must have been off."

"It didn't work," sobbed Yoshiko.

"What didn't work?"

"The poison."

Well, well, Adrian thought and lit a cigarette. He blew out the smoke carefully. The girl hid her face in her arms.

"Suicide?"

"Yes."

"And you wanted me to go along with you?"

"Yes. You wanted to, didn't you?"

He noted that she was using the intimate word for "you"; the shared experience of coming death had equalized them. A good thinker I am, Adrian thought. So we have studied philosophy and psychology have we? And Chinese literature thrown in? We have lived in the Far East for a number of years now. Hasn't it occurred to us yet that frustrated Japanese females like nothing better than double suicide? To walk the final plank, hand in hand with loverboy? A splendid obituary in the newspaper afterward, suitable mumblings at the university? Glory glory hallelujah. And he, subtle intellectual that he was, had handed her the thought himself, during that exotic evening spent in the inn's garden, between the paper lanterns. It would have been better if they could have made love first but because he, how stupid can one get, had insisted on telling her he was gay...asshole, Adrian thought.

"So what poison did you use?"

"Snake poison," sobbed Yoshiko. "I bought it at the

street market, from a witch. It would work slowly and painlessly, she said, but it's just another throwing-up brew, and she charged me so much money for it."

The sour smell emitted by her body made him back off a few feet more.

"Let's go for a swim."

"Without bathing suits?"

He stared at her unbelievingly. "Yes. Naked. You don't mind, do you, dear?" His voice was sharp with venom.

"I can't swim," Yoshiko said sweetly.

"Who cares? I only want you to wash up—you stink, you know. Why the hell did you have to drag me into this? Couldn't you at least have asked?" He shook her by the shoulders. "Moron. Even if I would be interested in suicide, couldn't you have granted me the grace of at least selecting my own place and time?"

"Don't you want to die, then?"

"What is that to you?" He pulled the blouse roughly off her shoulders and yanked on the thin belt of her skirt. The treatment seemed to please her. She dropped her arms and purred when he took off her bra and slip. He stepped out of his own clothes and pushed her toward the surf. He pushed too hard and she fell but he grabbed her arm and dragged her into the water before striking off on his own. When he swam back a few minutes later she was washing herself, dipping water daintily into her hands and pouring it down her back.

While swimming he had been able to reflect and find more reasons to be angry. He picked her up and threw her down on the beach. Professor de Roos raped his secretary Yoshiko, pushing roughly without giving her a chance to ease his way. He saw her eyes turn helplessly away and listened to her groaning with pleasure. The tremendous energy contained in his maleness took only a few thrusts before spurting into her; once his seed was released he pulled back and got up.

"That was that."

She smiled. "You're not gay at all."

He cursed her, using expressions he had picked up in low-class bars. What he said hurt; he saw the tremors in her body while he told her, as impolitely as possible, how much he despised her. "Ten of your type in exchange for one common whore, my slut, and you've no brains either. Your cleverest statements are based on common ignorance. You can only repeat parrot talk and even then you make mistakes. You should get married to whatever fool accepts your dowry and spend your time with a simple rice cooker, an on and off switch is about the only gadget you can handle. Stay out of my way and spare me your act. All you want to do is make an impression and all you come up with is a lousy imitation of some dumb movie star. Keep your saccharine to yourself and stay away from me."

She rolled away while he shouted at her. He followed her, kicking pebbles. He saw her hand reach into the hamper and come back holding a revolver. She aimed at his head. The barrel was short but heavy.

Extraordinary, Adrian thought, there are two slits on the sides of the barrel. I wonder why they were put in. But he knew that his mind was trying to ignore the problem and that the problem was pointed at him and that it was death.

"Idiot!" whispered Yoshiko. "And what do you imagine that I think of *you*? Eh? Now that I know that you aren't gay and that I'm not good enough for you." Her voice hissed. "Now I *hate* you. Your arrogance. Your egotism. I only wanted to be your friend. I never expected you to marry me. Foreigners always marry their own kind; they mate legally with pink hippos or giraffes. I knew that all along. You won't accept my gift. Take *this* gift." The revolver came a little closer.

"Calm down, Yoshiko," he tried to say calmly, but his words stuck together. The slightly trembling barrel and its large metal eye were annoying him by their persistence. If she fired, his entire head would come off. Jesus, what a wicked weapon.

"I'm quite calm," Yoshiko said pleasantly. "And I'll kill you first and myself later."

He saw her index finger move steadily. He also saw the plump heads of the bullets, mathematically grouped around the barrel, fixing him quietly. There was no shot, only a dry click. The ammo was old, probably. The thought flashed through his brain while he grabbed the revolver and twisted it out of her hand. He reached out to hit her but she was gone, climbing the hill behind her. A moment later he saw her again, pushing against an enormous rock.

Right, Adrian thought. If the poison doesn't work and the gun refuses I have to be smashed.

She came back, what else could she do? The rock weighed tons. She dressed, hiding behind the rock where she had vomited before. Her shoes were on the beach. He picked one up, walked to the boat, and pushed its thin strong heel through the bottom. The hole was quite small. He took the shoe back and dropped it next to the other.

He let her get in, pushed the oars into the boat, and shoved it into the water. She sat in the bow, looking away from him. He handed her her shoes, gave one last push, and walked back to the beach. The wind was blowing away from the island. He repacked the hamper, climbed the hill, and sat on the rock she had been pushing a few minutes ago.

The boat sank slowly. As he expected, she panicked and let go of the wreck, preferring to support herself on the floating oars. The boat drifted on, still showing its gunwales, carried by the buoyancy of its plastic material. He saw her head dip, come up a last time, and go under again.

She tried to kill me thrice, Adrian thought, and I only made one attempt, but I was successful, that's the difference. Three against one, that should equal things out. Or am I revenging my father after all? If that murder is added to what Yoshiko tried to do to me the scales should tip my way.

He lit a cigarette and noted that his hands were steady.

The boat man came an hour later, swishing over the little waves. He changed course and throttled his engine. He attached the wreck to his power boat and looked at the island. Adrian waved his white shirt.

"I had warned her," the boat man said, "those spiked heels penetrate a thin plastic hull easily. How come she was alone in the boat?"

"She wanted to row by herself for a while," Adrian said. "She claimed she had often rowed a small boat before. I went for a walk on the island and when I came back I saw that the boat was nearly sunk. *She* had disappeared altogether. It was too far to swim out. If I had tried I would have drowned myself."

"We'll have to telephone the police. I'm sorry about this misfortune. Did you know the girl well?"

"We were friends, not too close."

Now he'll ask me to pay for the boat, Adrian thought,

but the man said nothing. He bowed and pointed at the shore. "Shall we go?"

Guilt, Adrian thought as he got in. The flat powerboat flew over the lake, the fast movement cheered him up. Am I guilty? Of course I am. So will I even my guilt out by spending years and years in a small cell, on a diet of rice and wheat, boiled in water? That's what they serve in the jails here.

The boat approached the harbor. The engine behind him stuttered and coughed out.

No, Adrian thought. His hand slid into Yoshiko's hamper, grabbed the gun, appeared again, and dropped the revolver gently into the water. The boat man was checking his engine.

Adrian stepped on the shore. Boating, with a fatal end, that's how he would define this succession of events. The definition would be within acceptable truth. He would pass it to the police soon, and repeat his version for as long as he was questioned. No poison, no gun, no rock. No more than a simple, albeit tragic, accident, caused by the stubbornness of a stupid girl.

He would go home afterward, have a shower, smoke a cigar on the balcony of his apartment, and gloat.

He had to restrain himself not to laugh. He knew now what he was capable of doing if circumstances turned against him; the knowledge would be useful, undoubtedly. And Yoshiko? He shrugged his shoulders; he would forget her soon enough.

\\\\\\ 10 \\\\\\

SAITO VERSUS SATAN

FUJIYAMA CAME TO ATTENTION IN FRONT OF SAITO'S
desk and bowed deeply. The inspector gaped at his visitor.
"Yes, Sergeant-san?"

Sergeant Fujiyama's white hair contrasted well with
the pale olive of his tunic. He resembled one of the lesser
gods from the Confucianist pantheon; an incorruptible
immortal. He certainly deserved the comparison, especially in police headquarters where, from his exalted seat
behind the counter downstairs, he classified all incoming
cases. As far as Saito knew the sergeant had never been
seen away from the hall but here he was, bowing respectfully.

"Yes?" Saito asked again.

"A letter, Inspector-san."

The letter, in a plain envelope, slipped from the sergeant's hand onto Saito's blotter. The inspector opened
it as Fujiyama left his office, still bowing, walking back-
ward.

Saito studied the single sheet of thin rice paper, partly covered with brushed characters artfully touching each other. He hissed respectfully when he deciphered the signature. The chief-commissioner had only drawn his name, assuming correctly that his title and rank would be known. Saito glanced through the text.

Inspector Saito Masanobu will be fetched at seven P.M. at his house. His company will be appreciated by Gato.

Saito got up and looked out of the window. A barren branch brushing against the rough surface of a cemented wall provided little encouragement. He walked back to his desk. What could this mean? The invitation was an order. The order was an honor since Marquis Gato, chief of the Kyoto Municipal Police, had never stooped down to Saito's level before, not even through the official channels such as the offices of Commissioner Mitsu or Chief Inspector Ikemiya. The elegantly drawn message was a thunderbolt, cutting through all protocol.

Saito was sweating and he could feel the thumping of his heart. His hand moved slowly toward the pack of cigarettes near his telephone, touched it, and retreated again. He pulled a drawer of his desk with his other hand and produced an incense stick from a red lacquered box. He caught the stick in the V formed by his stretched thumbs and index fingers and bowed in the direction of a golden frame holding three snapshots. A moment later the incense smoldered in front of the portraits of his father, mother, and uncle. The two-dimensional faces fixed the descendant from their side of the death line. "I am alone," Saito whispered, "but you formed me, may I be worthy of your good thoughts."

While the smoke crinkled between him and the photos Saito tried to activate his brain. There seemed to be no cause for being fired. It was true that he had, by obstinate behavior and not generally accepted methods of detection, provided himself with a dubious reputation, but it was also true that he had solved every case allotted him during the three years that he worked for Homicide. He knew that he often irritated his immediate chief, Ikemiya, but he had reasons to assume that the usually bad-tempered and not too intelligent chief inspector rather liked his young assistant. Furthermore, Ikemiya benefited by Saito's efficient diligence. Nevertheless, whoever succeeds kicks against sore shins. It might very well be that sycophants had been spreading nasty rumors. and that the ill wind had found its way to the chief commissioner's spacious room on the top floor.

Will be fetched at seven P.M. at his house. Seven P.M. was outside working hours. *Fetched* sounded ominous but the expression could also have a polite connotation. Was he due for an evening on the town, in the company of an exalted personage? Did the inviting order contain a compliment? Saito wondered if some recent cleverness on his part was causing this commotion. The matter about the stamp had been past tense for a while and that other business with the suspect who made a mistake about a date had been considered by his superiors as a lucky shot.

Saito's glance connected with his mother's photo—she looked back indifferently. His father seemed tired, only Uncle smiled at him, from the peace of his moss garden that he had been tending daily for the last twenty years of his life. "What's up for me, Uncle?" Saito asked gently. "What am I getting myself into now?"

He could visualize the little old man while he heard the answer. Uncle Saito, dressed in his threadbare cotton kimono, leaning on his rake, grinned. "Whatever happens to you is unimportant—use your ever shifting position to detach yourself from illusion." Uncle had been a Zen-influenced hermit who started each day by chanting a sutra on the splendor of true insight, but he had also been a successful businessman and a celebrated philosophy professor.

The snapshots were lost in the incense smoke. Saito concentrated on the chief commissioner's letter again. What did he know about Gato? That he was of one of Japan's noblest families, knew the crown prince personally, visited the imperial court at least once a year. That he was some sixty years old, approaching retirement. Ex-naval officer, ex-politician. A tall man whose protruding stomach was camouflaged by the excellent cut of his suit; an aristocrat with a finely chiseled head, in which the main features were the thick brushed-up moustache and the heavy-lidded dark smoldering eyes. Wasn't there a rumor that Gato was also a literary genius, writing essays on early American literature under a pen name?

Saito smiled. He had seen Gato in Japanese dress once, during a New Year celebration at Headquarters. The Chief's impeccably correct silken kimono, his white socks, his *hakama*, the antique apron outdated gentlemen wear, had impressed the staff deeply. Ikemiya especially was moved. "Our Chief, Saito, represents our famed past. We may be proud that a man of his stature directs our efforts." Ikemiya usually hid his emotions but Saito had seen his superior's fleshy lower lip tremble. The stately figure presiding over the hall's stage had touched Ikemiya's soul, causing respect for all that is old and reliable. Gato's image fitted in with other cherished symbols—ancient graceful temples, Noh plays, the delicate shuffle of willowy geishas, the hesitant music of samisen and bamboo flute, the refined foods that titillate a nation during the festive days when it reflects on its glorious past and longevity.

Saito's smile changed into a smirk. I respect the gods, he thought, and maybe Gato is a living god, but I would prefer him to leave me alone. I had other plans for tonight.

There was little to do that day and Saito stayed behind his desk, musing as he perused reports. He went home at four and told his housekeeper about the event ahead. Old Mrs. Oba nearly folded double with awe. "Your bath, Saito-san, I will prepare it at once. You will have to shave too—I've just bought new razors. What will you wear? Your father's ceremonial robe? Your uncle's doesn't fit you and the holes show—I haven't been able to darn them well. He was always so careless with his tobacco."

"No, Oba-san, my British suit is good enough, and the necktie with the pink stripes."

She looked at him sadly. "I can't get the stains out; you spilled soy sauce on it."

"Any tie you care to select."

Saito took his time in the tub and slowly rubbed himself dry afterward. He put on a house robe and wandered into the altar room where he bowed to the tablets decorated with the names of his ancestors. Thinking that a mere bow did not fit the occasion he prostrated himself on the floormat before settling himself on his meditation cushions and forcing his legs into the lotus position. The cushions had belonged to his father and he didn't use them too often but today might be a day of change. Saito stretched his back and stared at a spot on the floor. Minutes passed while he tried to order his thoughts. Vaguely connected images haunted him and he regulated his breathing to work up enough strength to be rid of the disturbance. The restless thoughts joined into a clear vision of his uncle who, again in his garden, was lecturing his nephew. "Death approaches but you find me still busy, engaged in activities to which I deny all purpose."

"So why bother with them, Uncle?"

"For no reason, Nephew, for any reason I can come up with will pollute my emptiness."

"But everything you do, you do as well as you can, Uncle."

Uncle Saito scratched his chin with the handle of his rake. "Why not? When busy one might as well aim for perfection."

"Saito-san," Mrs. Oba called from the corridor, "you should get dressed."

"I'm coming."

He got up, prostrated himself in front of the altar again, and agreed with his uncle. "There is no purpose in this show of humility," he told his ancestors, "and even its gymnastic value is doubtful, but I enjoy greeting you all the same."

At seven sharp he was at his gate. At five past seven a Mazda sports car of the latest model slid past him, stopped, and reversed. Saito admired the low-slung vehicle. He had expected Gato to arrive in his service Toyota. The Mazda was of a class that is advertised in exclusive magazines, with foldout pictures that state no price. Saito estimated the amount and noted that it corresponded to a year's salary for top officials, expense account included.

The passenger door veered open and Saito stooped and got in.

"Evening, Saito," Gato said pleasantly. "I'm glad you could make yourself free. You haven't eaten yet, I hope."

"No, Gato-san." Saito saw with pleasure that his own

expensive suit looked shabby compared to the chief commissioner's elegant attire. "I appreciate the honor contained in your kind invitation."

"Be my guest," Gato said in English while he flicked the automatic gearshift and drove off soundlessly. "I've been told you speak good English, that's right, isn't it?"

"I didn't major in the language, Chief Commissioner-san, but I tried to do my best. My parents thought that Japan would fit in with the outside world more and more, and spoke English at home, in order to encourage me. They both completed their studies in America."

"Didn't you go there as well?"

"Only for a while, Chief Commissioner-san, as an exchange student."

The traffic light was red. Gato checked whether any traffic was coming from the side streets and drove on. "I agree with your honorable parents. If the high society of this country does not trouble itself to become bilingual we deny ourselves much pleasure. A knowledge of foreign languages will also benefit your career, but I don't have to tell you what you already know. You're a studious chap, I'm told. Aren't you after a Ph.D. in philosophy?"

"Yes, Chief Commissioner-san, but that's still a little ways off."

"Splendid. Don't be so formal, Saito, tonight we can ignore our ranks. What will it be? Sushi, tempura, or a good western steak?"

"I will be delighted to follow your choice."

"Not at all. You're my guest, but my information says that you prefer Japanese food and your housekeeper seems to be a local celebrity in gourmet cooking. Let's see if my friend Cheng can perhaps teach your Mrs. Oba a trick or two, eh?" Gato laughed.

Saito couldn't avoid reciting the commentary Gato's remarks provoked. "You know a lot about me, Gato-san."

"I have some training in detection," Gato said while he passed a city bus on the wrong side, "and I learned that one shouldn't only get to know suspects. Intimate knowledge of an assistant's lifestyle can be beneficial; it eases cooperation."

The Mazda crossed the Kamo River at the Maruta-machi Bridge and Saito looked aside to enjoy the contrast between the slow streaming water and gaily colored strips of cotton drying on the banks. A slender wooden craft poled by a young woman in country dress bobbed daintily in the current. Saito wanted to make a poetic remark but understood that Gato couldn't be appreciative of subtle wordplay at that particular moment. The Mazda was in the wrong lane again and only avoided an onrushing truck by the driver's sudden twisting of the steering wheel. I don't even drive like that when my siren and lights are on, Saito thought, and Gato's reactions must be slower than mine. The chief commissioner seemed able to handle the car, however, and Saito didn't feel too nervous—the Mazda's powerful engine should be able to save them from dangerous situations.

"Here, Cheng's Swallow Club, a pricey establishment perhaps, but whenever I eat elsewhere I realize my lack of good taste."

"Cheng? A Chinese?"

Gato parked and turned toward Saito. "By name only nowadays, although there must still be some Chinese blood in his veins. Cheng is a descendant of a great celebrity, Coxinga. himself. You're familiar with the name?"

"Cheng Ch'eng-kung," Saito answered obediently, "also known by his honorific title Kuo Hsing Yeng, which incorporates the imperial surname, but the Dutch could not pronounce the sound so they called him Coxinga instead. An adventurer, the son of a Chinese nobleman and a Japanese mother. Born here, near Nagasaki, if I remember correctly, in 1624 or thereabouts, and later a tyrant who, as a pirate, controlled the Strait of Taiwan. He even managed to conquer Taiwan, called Formosa then and a Dutch colony." Saito grinned. "A most popular figure in our and Chinese history but in reality a gangster of the first order."

Gato smiled. "Your formal education hasn't been wasted on you, Saito, and you certainly have a good memory. Yes, Cheng has a portrait of the great Coxinga between the tablets of his ancestors. When the Manchus took over China their hand lay heavily on Taiwan too and Coxinga's grandson fled to Japan. I'm glad he did for the present Cheng comes from that line and he's a most formidable man whose company has opened up interesting avenues for me."

"He's an innkeeper now?"

Gato had gotten out and held on to Saito's arm while they crossed the narrow street in the Willow Quarter. "So he seems to be, but the label covers a multitude of talents." Gato's arm gestured widely. "Most of this neighborhood belongs to him, and Cheng has other possessions, some fast cargo ships for instance, plying the seas between this country and Taiwan. When you and I know each other a little better his influence in many fields of activity will become clear to you. You might also be asked to admire his collection of Ming scrolls, the finest in the country, I'm told. Here we are, I better go in first to show our host he's dealing with the right guests. This is the establishment where he lives and it isn't exactly open to the public."

Saito bowed to the broad-shouldered portly man who received them in the club's small hall and thought of his uncle for a moment—an irrational association, perhaps, for Cheng and Uncle Saito were of different stature and bearing although the power they emitted might be of the same caliber.

"May I accompany the honorable guests to the upstairs room?" Cheng asked hoarsely. "I'm sorry that I'm not worthy to wait on you personally but the serving girls have been specially selected for your pleasure and I think that you will appreciate their company more than my clumsy presence."

"Ha," Gato said, "you do know how to twist words. By the way, it's about time we go pheasant hunting together again. The caretaker of my country home phoned yesterday to say that there are some fine birds about. Next week Saturday perhaps? I can pick you up."

Cheng smiled and bowed.

"Very well, I'll be here at nine A.M. Follow me, Saito, I know the way."

Saito had to admit that he had never eaten that well. The various courses appeared plain enough but their very simplicity hid their refinement, and a little herbal spice here and a touch of some exotic ingredient there added to a mosaic of delights that offered itself in heavenlike harmony. The girls were of the same order. They didn't seem, at first glance, to be particularly beautiful, but the perfect regularity of their features and their supple well-shaped bodies, accentuated by the unusually twisted hairdo of the one and the somewhat exaggerated eye makeup of the other, made their presence both sensuous and elegant. They behaved quietly, avoiding flirtatious banter, but their physical proximity while serving indicated clearly that they were available to any desire the guests deigned to express.

"Very tasty," Gato said, "and you are both delectable darlings, but my friend and I have a little business to discuss. Perhaps you should leave us to ourselves for a little while now. Saito, what do you think; shall we terminate the meal in the western fashion?"

The girls retreated, after having brought cognac and cigars.

"Right," Gato said. "Tell me, Saito, how did you manage Adirano Dorosu's untimely death the other day. I'm most curious to hear why the Dutch philosophy professor, mildly suspected of having murdered his secretary, chose to drink hemlock." Gato burped. "Ah, this was a delicious meal indeed."

Saito looked up. "Excuse me?"

Gato smiled. "Each report ultimately reaches my desk and although I don't read them all I've never missed studying one of yours. I will tell you why I find your method fascinating. You always research your situations impeccably and I know that your investigations usually result in an arrest. In the case of the drowned secretary I did not entertain that hope, for it was clear from the start that there were no indications of proof. You will understand that I have some experience in reading between the lines. You suspected Dorosu of murder although you did not say so clearly. You never arrested the professor either. I surmised you would not pursue the case, incorrectly as it turned out, for Professor Dorosu died yesterday, by his own hand." Gato burped again. "So let's hear how you brought him to that final decision."

Saito did not quite manage to hide a self-satisfied smile. Then he burped too.

"Well?"

Saito lit a cigar. "You must excuse me, Gato-san. I indulged too much and my brain is not clear. I'm afraid I cannot follow your line of reasoning."

Gato sipped cognac and smacked his lips contentedly. "Listen, Saito, I assure you that there are no hidden microphones in this room. I admire the way in which you handled the case, although my admiration may not be complete and I may have some criticism on a deeper level. That criticism, which I may express later, does not in any way outweigh the prize you're about to receive." Gato waved his cigar. "But I'm curious too and I insist that you answer my question. A little more cognac, friend?"

Saito's face was set. "No, thank you, I'd rather wait a moment."

Gato's smile broadened. "Very well, last things first then. Saito-san, I have the pleasure to inform you that you are promoted to inspector first class. You know that it's most unusual to jump from third to first class, especially for an officer as young as you are. However, your superior insight and diligence are clear to everyone at Headquarters. Even Sergeant Fujiyama has mentioned your name in a positive way several times already and in my experience that's a definite first. Ikemiya is backing you personally and has asked me for the favor of informing you himself but I suggested he should leave the matter to me. I work in a quiet room, Saito, and feel the need to communicate at times."

"Thank you," Saito said. The jubilance he had intended to express fell away. He saw Uncle Saito again. The old man squatted in his garden and pulled a small weed from the moss. *Whatever happens to you, Nephew, is not important. All that matters is that you use your circumstances to detach yourself from illusion.*

Gato surmised that the sudden acknowledgment of his superior qualities had unnerved the young man and that Saito had trouble in responding properly. The chief commissioner rubbed out his cigar. "Well, Inspector First Class-san, isn't one favor worth another? Don't forget that there should be no secrecy between colleagues and that both you and I are descendants of samurai. An extra code of honor binds us. The Dorosu solution is too mysterious for me and I need to know how you managed to fit your facts together in such a way that you could set off circumstances causing Dorosu to kill himself. Let me break up my query into certain clear-cut questions. How did you know that Dorosu did kill his secretary Yoshiko?"

Saito spoke monotonously, keeping his voice down, "I was faced by an intelligent opponent, who also happened to be a foreigner whose motivations, way of deciding, and potential activity were formed in an environment I'm not familiar with. As you said just now, the case provided insufficient proof and there was a complete absence of witnesses. If I wanted to pursue it, I would have to work as unobtrusively as possible."

"You suspected the professor immediately?"

"Only in theory, Gato-san. Dorosu spoke reasonably good Japanese but said as little as possible, preferring to let me listen to the man who rented him the boat. Whenever I asked the professor a direct question he either gave the shortest possible answer or just shrugged. He showed no emotion—an attitude that I could appreciate, for I knew the suspect and could therefore suppose that a man of his elevation would know how to control himself."

Gato looked surprised. "You knew him?"

"We had met at the university. He didn't know *me*, for he has many students and although I attended a number of his lectures he would not have noticed me." Saito smiled. "To us all foreigners resemble each other but we look alike in their eyes."

"Yes. According to your report you let Dorosu go home and asked the boat man to take you out to the island in his powerboat." Gato's nose wrinkled. "Out there you found certain traces, I believe."

"Yes, but I did not dwell on those in my report. I found vomit and excrement, smeared on two rocks, and deduced from the position of the rocks that the professor and the girl had been anxious to hide from each other while they were ill. I also found signs of a struggle or hectic love-making."

"And the imprint, on wet sand, of a gun."

"Yes, Gato-san. Later I also found the gun. By that time I had worked out a hypothesis that would fit the facts I had been able to locate."

"The revolver was found by a police diver, in the vicinity of the jetty. How did you know you would find it there?"

"I didn't, Gato-san, but there were only two spots where the diver could work profitably. He dived off the jetty and near the beach on the island."

"So you were lucky again."

Saito shook his head thoughtfully. "Not really, Gato-san. By that time I had collected more information, but as I still couldn't produce proof, I intended to stop wasting time and changed the direction of my inquiry. It's a well-known fact that women discuss the intimate side of their lives with girl friends. I study at the university myself which facilitated my next move. Discreet inquiries led me to the wife of one of the assistant professors, a young woman, some twenty years old, by the name of Suga, who was Yoshiko's close friend."

The cognac seemed to enthuse Gato. His laughter interrupted Saito's report. "That is indeed a good observation. My wife—you will understand that I didn't select her myself—used to have attractive bosom friends too, although she preferred the more homely variety later on. Pity for me as by then I had to begin looking for official concubines, an expensive pastime. But back to business, that Yoshiko was rather a plain duck, wasn't she?"

It took a few seconds before Gato's meaning penetrated to Saito's brain. "Yes, sir, but I believe Dorosu found her mind more repulsive than her body. Suga is a more attractive person and when I interrogated her, in a very offhanded way of course, it became clear that Suga was also interested in Professor Dorosu." Saito coughed. "As a fantasy. I don't think anything occurred between the two."

Gato nodded happily. "Exactly. Suga used her friend Yoshiko's confessions as substance for her own dreams. By the way, how attractive *was* Dorosu?"

Saito shrugged. "Hard to say, sir, I'm not a woman. He was tall, had blonde hair and blue eyes. An exotic man here, but I dare say he would be attractive to European women too."

Gato poured himself more cognac. "Blue-eyed demons we used to call them. But go on, so Suga was helpful, was she?"

"I was told," Saito said, "that the relationship between Dorosu and Yoshiko wasn't going too well but that Dorosu couldn't end it because he had to work with the girl. There had never been any real romance but Yoshiko knew that

Dorosu liked to drink and kept on taking him to bars. The couple also played a game; they discussed the possible purpose of human existence. Dorosu claimed that any existence is without purpose—"

"A Buddhist dogma," Gato interrupted.

"Yes, and Dorosu also posited that all life is suffering."

"Another slogan of the Buddhist creed."

"That's right, but Dorosu argued onward and thought he could prove that suffering can be prevented by refusing to accept life, and Buddhism never drew *that* shortsighted conclusion." Saito smiled apologetically. "Perhaps you do not care for this pillar of my hypothesis, Gato-san, but the suspect was a professor of philosophy and the subject therefore relates to our case."

"Go on, go on, your tale becomes more interesting all the time."

"Very well. Yoshiko wasn't too intelligent and swallowed any joke the professor cared to push her way. She thought he was perfectly serious when he told her that even the ancient Greeks, especially Socrates, whom he seemed to admire, had pointed out that man is potentially free—because man can refuse to live. The professor also misconstructed David Hume's theory. David Hume posited that ultimately nothing exists and that therefore all human values are fabricated. Here again Dorosu forced his witless disciple to accept that, because nothing matters, suicide is the only dignified way out."

Gato selected a fresh cigar. "You think he wanted her to kill herself so that he would be rid of her?"

"No," Saito said. "Not consciously anyway. He was only having his way with the girl, but he wasn't clever enough to see what the next step would be."

Gato had some trouble lighting his next cigar; he blew

on his finger where the match had burned him. "Double suicide, the stereotyped ending to any cheap romance, as shown on television."

"Yes, sir. Yoshiko was rather mysterious about her solution but her friend Suga guessed correctly what the silly girl was up to. My informant didn't worry too much, however, for she thought it unlikely that the professor would play the game to the end."

"So the construction became suicide plus murder."

Saito poured a little cognac into his glass and sipped carefully. "That was the idea but the poison didn't work. I understood that the gun had to belong to Yoshiko for why would Dorosu arm himself for a picnic? The gun was irrelevant, however, as it hadn't been used when I found it. I imagine that Dorosu got rid of it so as not to add unnecessary complications."

"We forget the firearm, Saito. *Then* what did you do?"

"Up till that moment I hadn't faced the suspect directly, apart from that original interview on the shore of Lake Biwa. It was time to meet Dorosu on a personal basis and Suga was kind enough to invite both the suspect and myself to a dinner party at her house."

Gato emptied his glass and reached for the bottle again. "That Suga shows up too often in your tale, Saito. How far did you have to go in order to secure her cooperation?"

Saito arranged the objects on the table. "She's married."

"So?"

"There's nothing between the lady and me, Gato-san. During dinner Dorosu and I talked to each other. He now knew that I wasn't only a philosophy student who sometimes attended his lectures but also the police inspector who asked him questions after Yoshiko's death. The combination didn't seem to worry him—he was friendly enough. I even got the impression that he rather liked me. My original theory was confirmed. Dorosu was rather a jolly fellow and not at all the manic depressive Yoshiko had made him out to be, in her own mind, and in her confessions to her friend. On the contrary, the suspect showed himself an intelligent and active man, eager to penetrate all sorts of mysteries, truly interested in philosophy, and well versed in literature. He could read Chinese and had picked up several thousands of our own characters, enough to read some of our modern writers in Japanese and—"

"Which authors did he like?" Gato asked.

"Tanizaki, mainly, and he had recently begun to read Kawabata."

"Which writer did he prefer?"

"Tanizaki."

Gato smiled knowingly. "Tanizaki, eh? So we may deduce that the professor was a bit neurotic, right? Liked the more bizarre aspects of the developed personality? Very well, your line of reasoning is becoming very clear."

Saito couldn't help grinning. "Yes, sir. I thought it might be worthwhile to instigate an experiment. One of the other guests at Suga's dinner party was a stage director who also teaches at the university. He told me that he often produces plays that have been written by the students, and I already knew that his work is appreciated by the staff and that many professors, including Dorosu, watched the performances. I therefore, during the following weekend, wrote a short play myself and changed my facts a little so as not to be too obvious My hero was a foreign manufacturer and I made the director choose a chubby student to play the part and insisted he should wear a brown wig. The lady in the play was rather beautiful, a classic-looking Japanese girl. But I did put in the picnic and I rather harped on the suicide/murder combination. The girl dies, the foreigner goes back to his country."

"Rather like the *Madame Butterfly* syndrome, right?"

"A little more realistically written, and acted, Gato-san."

Gato frowned. "Are you telling me that you made the girl shit and puke?"

"No, sir. She did vomit a little, but hidden behind a rock. The realism was contained in the rape scene, caused because the foreigner does not understand the subtle feelings of the girl. I made the dialogue rather coarse but I confess I inserted that bit to unmask the so-called daintiness of our women."

"Well well well," Gato said. "So you're a literary genius too. I should have made you a commissioner straight off. If I follow you correctly you intended to misrepresent what really happened sufficiently to make Dorosu still feel safe."

"Yes. I meant to make him look up in fear and then lull him back to sleep again. He had to be somewhat upset, however, to better knock him down later on that night."

Half a fifth of cognac and six or seven jugs of sake had not been the right combination for the chief commissioner. He no longer sat up straight, his movements were disconnected, and his eyes glowed somberly. "Carry on, Inspector First Class-san."

"Suga had provided me with photographs of Yoshiko and she also told me what clothes the secretary was wearing on the day she died. I selected three girls who had about the same posture as Yoshiko, and Suga helped me by applying the right makeup. Dorosu's habits were known to me. He would leave the theater, walk to the parking lot, then drive to a certain bar. I placed the three girls strategically. The first two were intended to be mere glimpses, so I asked one to stand near the door as he left the hall, and the second to cross the parking lot at the moment she caught sight of him. The third—"

"One moment," Gato said, waving his cigar. "They were dressed like Yoshiko. Who paid for the clothes?"

"I did, sir. The third girl was waiting in the bar. So was I. Dorosu saw me when he came in and greeted me but I pretended not to see him. He saw the girl too. She was in the company of Sergeant Kobori."

"Was the sergeant in uniform?"

"No, sir."

"Why did the sergeant have to be there?"

"I was concerned about the girl's safety, sir. By that time Dorosu should have been badly shaken."

"You think he might have attacked her?"

"I'm not sure, but if he had, Kobori and I would have been able to take care of the situation."

"Hmm. Creating nasty visions, eh? Where did you get that idea?"

Saito rubbed his chin. "I first came across the method in an old manual on detection, *Parallel Cases Under the Pear Tree*, a thirteenth-century Chinese book."

"I've heard of it. The old magistrates used living corpses?"

"Sometimes, sir. They would also dress themselves up as judges of the netherworld and suddenly appear in the suspect's cell. There would be eerie music and so forth. The prisoner had been physically and mentally prepared for the ordeal, by torture usually."

Gato's long hair was hanging in his eyes. He brushed

it back impatiently. "Torturing is out of fashion nowadays, but you're getting close to it again. However, no matter. What exactly were you trying to achieve?"

"Break the professor's defenses. Destroy the wall he had built to protect himself from his own hell. Conscience, especially, perhaps, in an intelligent and cultured man, is subconscious, and only shows itself in moods and dreams. By involving Dorosu in a *conscious* dream I meant to activate his guilt."

"Hm."

Saito didn't notice the objection. "What I really meant to find out, it seems to me now, is whether morals are valid. If Dorosu hadn't reacted the way he did I might have come to the tentative conclusion that we are allowed, under certain circumstances, to kill an antagonist whose behavior we interpret as obnoxious and irritating."

Gato played with his glass. "So, a few days later, Professor Adirano Dorosu drank the juice of the hemlock root, in a hotel room in Otsu, with a view of Lake Biwa. A suitable location selected by himself this time, or are you going to tell me that you managed to send him to that exact spot?"

"No, Gato-san, the final choice was his."

Gato shook his head. "Why that strange poison? I had never even heard of it. Some Dutch concoction maybe?"

Saito's grimace expressed sadness. "It killed Socrates, sir, and Socrates was the professor's preferred philosopher. It can be bought at the street market, where the druggists sell it as mouse poison. It paralyzes the body slowly, causes no pain, and death comes like a soft and luxurious blanket."

"Good," Gato said. "Very good. Worth considerable praise." The chief commissioner made an effort to sit up properly. "But now I will tell you what I have against your way of handling this case. I would say that you have allowed yourself too much youthful enthusiasm and have not considered the merits of the case sufficiently. You're a police officer and the state has entrusted you with applying the law, but you should know that the law makes unwritten exceptions. Dorosu was an exceptional man. That he also happened to be a foreigner supplies some excuse and therefore I shan't be too hard on you." Gato's index finger prodded Saito's arm. "Listen here, Saito, you and I are samurai, and Dorosu had the same status in his own country. I mean to say that he, by his intelligence, education, and general bearing had managed to reach the highest possible human level, and I will prove to you that the law does not reach those lofty heights."

Saito's mouth dropped open. "But—"

"Let me finish. Do you happen to know Aldous Huxley's book *Brave New World*?"

"I read it."

"So did I, many years ago now, and it fascinated me, but not in the way the author intended. Huxley was a typical constrained example of his time, a most limited thinker. He describes the difference between common man and advanced man, and does it correctly. I recall that his superior men were *Alpha* types and that the common varieties were subdivided into *Beta*, *Gamma*, et cetera. The latter types are genetically manufactured and programed in a limited way so that they can function optimally in given situations. Only Alphas are free to enjoy life. Correct?"

"I remember, Gato-san."

"Very well. And that wouldn't be the right way of doing things, according to nice Mr. Huxley, and that wrong thought makes his book uninteresting." Gato's lecturing seemed to give him new strength and he no longer slouched on his cushions. "I tell you, Saito, Huxley saw some truth, but failed to explain it, to either himself or his readers. You and I, and Dorosu, are near-perfect men, and the others are not, they are Huxley's Betas and Gammas. That doesn't only go for Japan but for all countries. I know, for I have traveled widely. The Alphas have different names—in America they're called capitalists, in China officials and army officers, in Russia party members, in other countries something else again—but they are around today, and not in the science fiction realm Mr. Huxley predicted."

Saito was staring wide-eyed at his chief.

Gato laughed. "You still don't believe me? Look around you, Inspector-san. Take your own assistants. Your dutiful, dutybound I should say, Sergeant Kobori for instance—have you ever met with a more exemplary Beta? A programed man if ever I saw one, an obedient slave. And what about Sergeant Fujiyama, isn't he an even better example of what our tradition can create in the way of small-mindedness? Have you ever visited one of our car factories, where the laborers line up in the morning to chant the Toyota song before they start work? All societies have created that situation, which benefits us, and all societies were always led by us."

Saito found his tongue. "I'm not aware of that, sir."

Gato smiled lovingly. "That's why you are here tonight. I have to initiate you. You were born an Alpha, Saito, but you're not aware of your privileged position yet."

Gato filled Saito's glass. "Initiation is a difficult process. I take it the light I've passed to you is blinding you at the present moment. You're twenty-nine years old and your position as first class inspector gives you considerable power now. There'll be more power later on, by the time you're forty you should have my present rank. All Japan will be your playground then, and a good part of the rest of the world, wherever you care to go. The others will work while you study, observe, understand, enjoy. You won't be alone, however; there are other Alphas around you, samurai, V.I.P.'s, whatever they may be called by the lower denizens." Gato paused for a moment. When he spoke again he looked very serious. "You shouldn't be killing your peers and brothers, you shouldn't be breaking the code. What you did to Dorosu was a mistake. Don't repeat it."

"You're joking, sir."

"Not at all." Gato wanted to hit the table but his hand slid off its edge and his torso tottered. He managed to right himself again. "Not at all, Saito. But I'll give you the time to let my words sink in. If you want to be my disciple and successor you will have to see the error of your present way. That you have been promoted already shows my trust in your perception. I also admire your diligence, but in the case we just discussed it was misdirected."

Saito sipped quietly. Gato raised his own glass and laughed. "Don't look so bewildered. You'll soon realize what possibilities I'm offering to you. Enough of this now, it's time for other pleasures. Let's call the charming ladies and ask them to show us the way to the bedrooms upstairs." Gato checked his watch. "Midnight exactly, a propitious moment. I will meet you again at two A.M. at the front door."

* * *

Saito pulled the pillow under his head so that he could have a better view of the girl, who was taking her clothes off at the other side of the room. She was timing her performance to the beat of a slow blues song flooding her cozy quarters from speakers hidden in the walls. When the record clicked off, she approached the bed, pulled the sheets away, and nestled in Saito's arm.

Saito tried to perform well but he was drunk and kept dozing off. At twenty to two his electronic watch jangled him awake. The girl was caressing his hair. "You have to leave? What a pity, you're such a good lover. Will you be coming back again soon?"

Saito dressed. He smiled at the girl. "Would you do me a favor?"

"Anything you say."

"Call Mr. Cheng for me, please. Tell him that Inspector Saito, of the Kyoto Municipal Police, would like to speak to him."

She sat up and embraced her knees. "You were not happy with my company? Please do not complain about me."

Saito squatted and lit a cigarette. "You're a beautiful and thoughtful girl and satisfied all my wishes. But please fetch Cheng-san. I have a little business to discuss with him."

"You wished to see me?"

Saito got up from the bed and nodded at the bowing innkeeper.

"Yes, Mr. Cheng. I would like to pay."

Cheng bowed again, rather clumsily, and his hands slid out of the sleeves of his robe. He showed his palms, as if he wanted to defend himself. "It's an honor to me to be allowed to receive the high-placed Gato-samma and his appreciated colleague in our lowly establishment, Inspector-san. Your continuing protection is worth more to us than we will ever be able to show in our simple and uneducated ways. I do hope that you have been able to relax a little tonight."

"I have no complaints at all," Saito said. "But please tell me, appreciated host, how much this evening's pleasure would have cost me if I had come without the chief commissioner's introduction?"

Cheng's large hands fluttered. "How can I discuss such a despicable detail with somebody of your lofty level?"

"I'm a curious student of life," Saito said. "Please mention the price."

Cheng whispered the amount and wanted to turn toward the door but Saito raised his voice. "One moment, Mr. Cheng. Allow me to give you a gift, in return for a receipt."

Cheng no longer smiled. "You're insulting me, Inspector."

"I'm sorry if I do. Here's the money." Saito tore a page from his notebook and offered a pen. "The receipt please, Cheng-san."

Commissioner Mitsu nodded from behind his desk and indicated two chairs. "Good morning, Ikemiya-san." He beamed at Saito over his half-glasses. "And what do we have here, our recently baked new inspector first class in person? My congratulations, Saito."

Saito bowed deeply before he sat down.

Commissioner Mitsu pushed away the paper that Chief Inspector Ikemiya had placed on his desk. "I've already glanced at a copy of the report. A nasty business, Ikemiya. So what happened exactly?"

Ikemiya hissed politely. "I will tell you, Mitsu-san. This morning, at about 2:30 A.M., Chief Commissioner Gato and Inspector Saito left the Swallow Club in the Willow Quarter, the inn belonging to Cheng-su. Both gentlemen had been drinking. The chief commissioner refused to get into a cab stopped by Saito as he wished to use his own car. Saito argued with the Chief but Gato-san insisted and finally ordered his subordinate to drive with him in his private car. When the car, the Mazda convertible Gato-san bought some months ago, reached the river and turned toward the bridge the vehicle hit a pedestrian who was standing on the sidewalk of the Kamo Boulevard. The pedestrian, a certain Mr. Tagawa, a shopkeeper of this city, died instantaneously. The Mazda then hit a lamp post but the driver and his passenger were unhurt. A squad car arrived and Corporal Subu wrote the report you have already read. He noted that Gato-san was not sober and suggested a blood test which the Chief refused. Gato-san, in view of his exalted rank, was not arrested and was allowed to go home in a taxi."

Commissioner Mitsu polished his glasses with his handkerchief. "The Chief just telephoned. He doesn't feel well and is not coming in today."

"I'm sorry to hear that," Ikemiya said mechanically. "Corporal Subu stated that the Mazda must have been speeding and quotes the nature of the tire marks on the road as evidence."

"Very well, Ikemiya, so what do we do now?"

Ikemiya massaged his sagging chin. "Bad business, Commissioner-san. The Chief refused a blood test, which makes him legally drunk. Driving under the influence is a crime by itself and the death of Tagawa gets him into manslaughter. The report should be sent to the attorney general forthwith and we should meanwhile arrest the suspect." Ikemiya dropped his hand. "Under normal circumstances..."

"But the circumstances aren't normal. What do you suggest our action should be?"

Ikemiya turned ponderously and looked at Saito.

Saito nodded. "I know Corporal Subu well," he said to the commissioner, "as a colleague and as a member of the karate club. The chief inspector thought I should contact the corporal and request that he rewrite his report."

"And are you willing to do that?"

"No, sir. I don't think an exception should be made, and I don't, if you'll excuse me, agree that there should be any special circumstances."

Commissioner Mitsu turned and held up his glasses, checking them against the sunlight. "Why should I excuse you? I take it that you have attempted to consider the case in a proper manner." He put on his glasses and smiled at Saito. "You understand what we have here, Inspector. Your course would bring shame on the Chief and therefore shame on the police."

"If the case would go to court, sir."

"You see a way of preventing that course of events?"

Saito didn't react. The commissioner looked at Ikemiya. Ikemiya stared at the floor.

The room's silence was interrupted by a ticking noise at the window. The commissioner produced a tin, shook some crumbs on his hand, and opened the window. He dropped the crumbs on the outside window-sill and closed the window again. "My friend the sparrow," he said softly. "We have an agreement. He chirrups for me and I feed him." He sat down. "I assume your mind is made up, Saito, and that there is no point in begging you to change it. I will visit the chief commissioner at once." He nodded at his visitors. "You can go, gentlemen."

The investigation regarding the chief commissioner's tragic death was conducted by Commissioner Mitsu. The commissioner was assisted by Chief Inspector Ikemiya and Inspector First Class Saito.

Mitsu bowed to Mrs. Gato, who received the gentlemen in the receiving room of her large villa on the southwestern side of the city. "Your husband decided to end his life, Mrs. Gato, and his motivation is clear to us. The poison he used is somewhat unusual, however. Could you tell us perhaps how your husband obtained the hemlock juice?"

The lady knelt stiffly on the floormat, exactly in between its richly ornamented border strips. She looked away. The three policemen were kneeling too, on the cushions that had been brought by a younger woman. Saito studied the woman for a moment. He suspected that she would be Gato's first concubine. The elegant style of the dwelling reminded him of Cheng's Swallow Club but the villa was more stately than the inn. He supposed that Mrs. Gato's personal style would account for the difference in atmosphere. He looked back at the small stiff lady with the gray hair, dressed in a somber kimono held by a purple obi. It seemed as if the wide silk waistband shielded not only her body but her soul as well.

Mrs. Gato's narrow hand beckoned the young woman who was standing behind the policemen. "Miya-san?"

Miya knelt next to the mistress of the house, a little to the rear. She adjusted the folds of her colorful kimono before she directed herself to the visitors. "The master sent me to the market yesterday morning to buy the medicine."

"Medicine?" Commissioner Mitsu asked. "You weren't aware that the substance is poisonous?"

"No, Commissioner-san."

"The master drank the poison in your presence?"

"Yes, and afterward he asked me to please fetch the mistress."

Mrs. Gato spoke in a soft voice. "My husband told me what had happened. I stayed with him. He said that the feeling in his legs had gone and that the paralysis was spreading to his chest. When the hemlock reached his heart he died quietly."

"You called the doctor?"

"Afterward, Commissioner-san. My husband had old-fashioned ideas; they weren't all correct but this one was. I'm sorry he left me but I respect his final decision."

"Old-fashioned ideas," Commissioner Mitsu said during the drive back to Headquarters. "Perhaps the solution we thought of wasn't too modern either. It isn't commonly applied in the world outside our islands. It seems that modern thought requires a man to take responsibility for his sins, not in a later life, but right now."

Ikemiya was staring at the ragged smoke coming out of the exhaust of the bus that drove ahead of the police car. "As you say, Commissioner-san."

"And what does our inspector think?"

Saito shook his head.

Commissioner Mitsu smiled. "You look somewhat pale, Saito. I would suggest that you take a few days off."

⫸⫸⫸ 11 ⫷⫷⫷

SAITO VERSUS SAITO

COMMISSIONER MITSU PICKED UP HIS TELEPHONE. "Yes?"

A hoarse voice whispered its message. "Detective Soseki, sir. I brought him in."

"Where is he now?"

"In his office."

"And why did it take you so long?"

The sounds produced by the detective weren't clear. Commissioner Mitsu interpreted them as a possible combination of sardonic giggling and polite throat rasping. "To find him," Soseki said when he was ready to speak again, "wasn't too hard, Commissioner-san, but he wasn't in good shape."

"He is now?"

"Not quite, sir."

Saito sat behind his desk and waited impatiently for his tea water to boil. The electric hibachi wasn't working well. The inspector's hands trembled when he unscrewed the top of a tube of aspirin and inserted two tablets between his cracked lips. The telephone rang. He hurriedly poured some lukewarm water, swallowed the tablets, and grabbed the phone. "Yes?"

"Mitsu here. I hear you have returned. How do you feel?"

Saito tried to move his tongue, it seemed stuck to his palate.

"Saito?"

"Yes."

"Are you ill?"

"Yes."

"I'm sorry to hear that but I'd like to see you all the same. I'll be here, waiting for you. Take your time, Inspector-san."

Mitsu looked at the crushed figure that had retreated as far as possible into the leather-upholstered easy chair. "I'm sorry I had to send out a search party, but your housekeeper was worried and telephoned a few times and I do have some experienced detectives at my disposal after all. The Willow Quarter is not a hermitage, Saito. I had hoped that you would have used your time off to rest."

Saito's bloodshot eyes stared dully at the commissioner.

"I couldn't rest."

"Would you tell me why not?"

"That won't be necessary. I have decided to resign from the force."

Mitsu got up. "Well, if you consider yourself to be a free citizen again I can't apply pressure, can I?" The commissioner took a cup from a side table and filled it from a small porcelain pot. "But I can still offer you a refreshment; this is the bitter variety that is reputed to take excellent care of hangovers. Drink up, Saito."

Saito emptied the cup in one draught and held it up again. Mitsu refilled it. "There's the pot, if you want more help yourself. Alcohol dehydrates the body, they say." The commissioner smiled. "But why did you insist on finding refuge in the bottle? Isn't that rather an easy way out?"

Mitsu's kind soft voice finally penetrated. Saito made an attempt to focus his eyes and his hand strayed to the breast pocket of his soiled shirt. "Can I smoke?"

"But of course." Mitsu waited till Saito had lit his crumpled cigarette. "Now will you tell me why you preferred the Willow Quarter to the peace of your parents' home?"

"My parents are dead."

"I know."

"Uncle Saito is dead too."

"Yes," Mitsu said. "Do you know that your uncle and I were acquainted? A long time ago, before he retired to Suyama. We studied at the same university but he was almost finished when I arrived. Your uncle was much admired because of his energy and enthusiasm."

Saito had expected a severe scolding and planned to let the criticism pass before leaving the room calmly. Mitsu's fatherly approach was too much for him. He began to talk, interrupting and repeating himself, mumbling incoherently sometimes. Mitsu listened.

Saito left nothing out. Three days of continuous intoxication, three nights in cheap hotel rooms where he couldn't sleep but watched the ceiling, paralyzed by fatigue, had destroyed his normal brightness but had also offered glimpses into what was happening in the recesses of his mind, in the semi-darkness that, up till now, he had been able to avoid. He finally ran out of words, and looked at his muddy shoes.

Mitsu left his protected position behind the majestic desk, pulled up a chair, and sat down opposite Saito. "Thank you. I'm glad you were willing to talk after all. That you intend to resign does not interest me at the moment; you can fill out the necessary forms downstairs when you leave here. What goes on within you does concern me, however, mainly because I recognize the process. You have failed, you seem to think. Isn't that what you were trying to tell me?"

"Yes."

"And you failed because of your own arrogance, isn't that the way to put it?"

"Yes."

Mitsu stretched his short legs and folded his hands on his protruding stomach. "That's the way I have often felt, and I can tell you that I haven't come to the end of my conflict either. We have a most unusual profession, Saito. Around us the maelstrom roars, the never-ending turbulence that disturbs society's peace, and we're sucked down even while we are trying to do our job. We perceive the criminal's thoughts because they are our own, for we all share the shadow that forever darkens the environment."

"I murdered twice," Saito whispered.

Mitsu's right hand disappeared under his jacket and came back holding a small model pistol. He showed the weapon to Saito. "You still have yours?"

"Yes."

"Carrying a firearm is illegal, but it's our duty to break that rule. There are even situations when we are obliged to shoot at a suspect, and shoot to kill. That means that the state has placed us in an exceptional position and wants us to behave in an irregular manner." Mitsu replaced his gun. "Dorosu was a murderer, and our law prohibits taking the life of another. He was also a scholar, and reputed to be a genius. You admired him when you attended his lectures since he represented your own intelligence, your own talent for logical argumentation. But he also symbolized the arrogance of your intelligence."

"Yes."

"But didn't you rather only try to destroy your own shadow? Do you remember what you said a few times just now, *that all that matters is that we should learn to be detached from what seems to be happening to us*?"

"That's what Uncle Saito said."

"Certainly, and he was right, but it was easy for him to state the truth in the peace of his retirement in Suyama. I think I've listened to you well, Saito. You were disturbed while you talked to me but you seemed to relax whenever you mentioned Suyama. In the past you've only been able to gain peace when you stayed with your uncle. I have already told you that I used to know him, when he was still young. He very much resembled you then, the way you are now. I can assure you that it took a long time, and much effort, for your uncle to reach the lofty position from which he could influence you when you went to stay with him."

Saito had straightened up a little.

Mitsu walked back to the other side of his desk. "You still own his house in Suyama?"

"Yes, Commissioner-san."

"Is anyone living there?"

"No, I've been thinking of selling it."

"You have been keeping it as a museum? That is good. But museums need to be visited from time to time. Your sick leave isn't over yet, I think you should go there and take your housekeeper with you. You can stay as long as you like, a week, a month perhaps."

"My resignation..."

Mitsu picked up the teapot. It was empty. He picked up his telephone. "Tea, please." The receiver clicked back into its holder. "You can consider your resignation when you return. In Suyama your uncle's spirit is waiting for you. What did he do out there?"

"He chanted sutras in the early morning, worked in his garden, read a little at times."

"You can do the same. Find the strength of your peace." Mitsu's small strong hand played contentedly with the thick golden watch chain that adorned his waistcoat. "But peace can become monotonous for someone who still has youthful energy."

A constable brought a dented tin teapot and filled the commissioner's and Saito's cups. Mitsu smacked his lips. "That cheap brew they make downstairs is quite invigorating at times. Yes, Saito, if all that peace and quiet should become too much for you down at the coast you can reflect a little about what keeps us busy here. Not too much of course, but a little interest might not harm you."

"You have a special subject in mind, Commissioner-san?"

"Ah, the brain is functioning again I see. Tell me, Inspector, when you wandered about the Willow Quarter, did you notice anything?"

"Not too much, Commissioner-san."

"Not too much, eh? Well, alcohol and perception do not always go together. But even so, I do remember that, in the time I used to indulge, I did pick up certain things, and quite clearly sometimes."

"Like what for instance, Commissioner-san?"

Mitsu's expression had hardened. "Like Cheng, Saito. Cheng-su the owner of the Swallow Club, the black demon who controls the Willow Quarter." It seemed that the commissioner was taken aback by his own sharp voice. He took off his spectacles and breathed on the lenses. "You did meet with him, didn't you?"

"Yes, sir."

"So did I, about five years ago. I even arrested him, on a charge of illegal importation and trafficking in dangerous drugs. Taiwanese heroin. Cheng-su has good connections out there, and he goes to the island quite often."

"You released him again?"

"The chief commissioner wanted to take care of the case and whatever occurred from then on passed me by. A while ago our detectives picked up a fresh trail and traced it to Quemoy. Quemoy is a small island and belongs to Taiwan. The line also connected with the Swallow Club."

"You pursued the facts?"

"I have done nothing so far."

"The chief commissioner . . . ?"

"I did not want to disturb Gato-san."

Saito was almost sitting up.

Mitsu replaced his glasses. "You know Cheng-su personally. He has even received you hospitably in his inn. The suspect likes to entertain police officers. I trust you had a good time?"

"I paid, Mitsu-san."

"Cheng-su is known to refuse payment from police officers." Saito pulled his wallet from his inside pocket and fumbled in its fold. He produced a folded bit of paper. "Please look at this receipt, sir."

Mitsu studied the crumpled little sheet. "Very well, I had hoped as much. You didn't slide into the trap. Some of your colleagues have and I cannot use them for this particular investigation."

Saito got up. He stumbled and held on to Mitsu's desk. "Perhaps..."

The commissioner forced himself to smile "Not yet, Saito. Go to Suyama, take your time. You will remember that one of our constables shot a dangerous and armed lunatic earlier this year. The suspect was dead by the time the ambulance picked him up. Sergeant Fujiyama suggested that the constable should go fishing for a couple of weeks, but the man was sent back on street patrol. A little while later that same constable tried to arrest a lady who was suffering of an attack of nerves. She was throwing empty bottles out of her window. The lady threatened the constable with a kitchen knife. The constable shot her through the head."

Saito let go of the desk and bowed. When he straightened out again his eyes were closed and sweat poured down his forehead. "I'm on my way to Suyama, Commissioner-san. Thank you. I will report back in due course."

Mitsu watched the door close. Something ticked against his window and he turned. "There you are," he said to the sparrow, "I had forgotten all about you." He opened the window and the sparrow eyed him expectantly. "Have you been chirping for nothing?" Mitsu asked. "Here, a bit late, but these are good crumbs.

"Maybe I've been chirping for nothing too," he mumbled when he had closed the window again. "Although I don't think I have this time."